Aden
The Beginning

Aden
The Beginning
Tiffany D. Young

TiDa Publishing
2015

Copyright © 2015 by Tiffany D. Young

All rights reserved. This book or any portion thereof may not be reproduced or used in any manner whatsoever without the express written permission of the publisher except for the use of brief quotations in a book review or scholarly journal.

First Printing: September 2015

ISBN 978-1-329-51763-9

TiDa Publishing
25136 Potomac Dr.
South Lyon, Michigan 48178

Dedication

To the One above

Thank you.
Without you this could not be possible.

Acknowledgements

I would like to thank everyone who believed in me and my writing. To everyone who have encouraged me to keep going and to not give up. To my parents David and Debra, my brothers Daris, David and William. My little cousin Jasmin, and my friends Karen, Echo. I love you all. Also, to everyone who have been patiently waiting all these years. No one has pushed me harder then you all and never let me quit even when I was ready to throw in the towel. I am happy that you all are a part of my life.

Aden The Beginning

Chapter 1: A New World

The professor walked around passing out packets to the class and in bold print it said "Final Project" I couldn't help but sigh. My classmates were talking to one another about this assignment. "Ok, settle down." The professor said. "The art teachers from this school belongs to the Design Town Corporation. This organization sponsors young talented artist around the country." He held a piece of paper in his hand. "Design Town wants to put their first building in Michigan and will dedicate it to the students in the universities all over." The class clapped, they all were excited. It was amazing. "They are giving us the freedom to find and decorate the building. Once we purchase a building with the check they have sent, the CEO's and managers will visit the finish product." He said. The teacher's want to make this a challenge for the students. You will be responsible for finding a building and researching it for a perfect studio for classes. Pick a partner, two people to a group and show your creativity with your own designs. Take plenty of pictures, and have the history of the building. Read these papers carefully and get to work. Projects are due in three weeks." The class was dismissed. The semester was coming to an end, and final projects were underway. My name is Gina and this is my designing class that I take with my best friend Maggie and it's the beginning of every tortuous Tuesday. It is so demanding and takes away a lot of energy. It's draining to talk all morning, before working on projects.

"Can you believe we have two days off from this class?"

"Thank God, I'm so sick of this class Maggie, everyday it's more research." I said.

"Where are we going to eat? Three hours of this guy makes me hungry." Maggie said.

"Gina. Maggie. You ladies know you're standing in front of the classroom door?" The teacher smiled walking down the hall.

"Sorry!" I was embarrassed. Maggie and I laughed.

After lunch we started immediately searching. We are excited for this assignment. We found Vicki, a Real Estate Agent and we communicated our budget for a building and followed the instructions in the packet. Vicki had a few places she could show today. The first place was a house made into a office space. It was too expensive. The second place there wasn't enough parking and it was built with no way out we would have to pay to have entrances and exits. The final building had blue panels, and limited on appearances, a perfect area, but it was an old building. This place wasn't that far from the school. It had double steel doors, but I imagined glass doors. The building had a gorgeous fresh brick look, but trashed laid scattered all around. There was some graffiti on the building that looked like crazy eyes on a smiling cartoon character. The double steel doors had dents in it from what looked like a hammer. Vicki had mentioned the building was broken into a few times and the side doors needed repairing. Her phone rang and she needed to answer it so Maggie and I entered the building.

"This place is creepy Gina. Do you even want to consider this for our project?" Maggie said.

"This will be excellent. With some sprucing, it will be great and cheaper than one fixed already." I said to Maggie as I walking through the building. There was Spider webs and broken floor boards everywhere. This place has potential. I notice the beauty, while Maggie shut her eyes. We separated, I went down one hallway as Maggie entered another. This building had six rooms, a great size front area restrooms for men and women. I walked towards the back. I saw candles burning and it was obvious someone lived here. Part of me wanted to warn Maggie, but I gravitated towards the room like a magnet. It was gloomy and the walls were gray with high ceilings that appeared gold, and I squinted my eyes because of the glare. The borders were dark and the floor sparkled like diamonds. There's beauty that revealed itself in this run down place.

Walking through this room brought a smile to my face. I noticed stacks of books along the walls, many that I owned myself. The beautiful silks that covered the bed blew my mind with the different colors, the warm and soft feel of it. This couldn't have been the same building. I could hear Maggie discussion in the front, I heard what was being said even though my interest was on the person staying here, alone in the dark. Why am I drawn to the things laying before me? "What are you doing in here?" A strange and powerful voice asked Maggie. I stayed in thought focusing on the room. "Sir are you okay? I see your injured can I help you?" There was a problem. I tried to pull myself from the back area, but I was captivated. I notice something strange by the bed. "No, get out." The voice demanded and was a bit terrifying. I wanted to move but I stood frozen. "My name is Maggie and my friend Gina is here we can get you help." Maggie said. It was a disturbing picture in a frame of a creature or a man on fire. It seemed every bit of three-hundred pounds, but healthy and muscular. I continued to listen to the conversation in the front, but I didn't move. The man's face in the picture didn't appear pained, he looked calmed as if the flames were normal to him. I wondered what person would frame this work. I began heading to the front. "He must be an artist." I said, I felt myself spacing out into many reasons because this picture was taken of a real person on fire, how did they do this? Before my thoughts could progress...

"Get the hell out." The words echoed through the building. I could hear shatter glass and a loud scream. This jolted me from my infatuation with the room.

"Maggie!" I ran towards the sound looking for her. Panic had come over me, the separate rooms are like being in a maze. My heartbeat rapid because she was nowhere to be found. "Maggie!" I repeated, but she didn't answer and I couldn't find her. She appeared out of the dark. "Are you okay, what's wrong?"

"I . . . it's! Something's here . . .!" Maggie said crying. She seem out of breath as she held onto me looking around. She made sure to glance behind her.

"Slow down. What did you see?" I asked as the realtor entered in the room.

"Are you alright? What happened?" Vicki asked looking at Maggie.

"I don't like this place, a guy, or... It's something in here Gina. He wasn't normal. Let's leave." She said trying to pull herself together.

"What did he look like?" I asked, looking around.

"He had scars, cuts, and blood everywhere. Gina let's go." Maggie said.

"Ok, let's leave and I will call the cops." The realtor said pushing us out.

Maggie walked out of the building and a shadow appeared across the room, with a hooded cloak, but it vanished. I stood looking to see if I was just imagining things. I told myself, "Stop being curious Gina." I shook my head and walked out. We were in the car driving home, and Maggie didn't say a word, as a matter of fact not an utter at all since we left. I wonder what was going through her mind... She said a guy? And I saw candles burning and belongings all over the place. "Are you okay Mag?" I asked.

"Yeah, a little shaken, but I'm okay." She responded.

"I saw candles burning in the back room, and personal items. Some guy maybe living there and tried to scare you away when he notice you."

"Well, why didn't you run straight out and warn me?" She asked.

"I was making my way back to you when you screamed." I replied, a little lie.

"There's something wrong with that guy. He was shaking, and when he yelled, which freaked me out and all the blood everywhere. I asked him was he alright and then he looked at me."

"Maggie, wow! It sounds like he could have been in bad shape. Maybe we should go back and help him." I said.

"No, I'm not going back. He seemed crazy. Plus the realtor and cops will take care of it"

"Wouldn't you want someone to help you if they saw you in his predicament?"

"Gina, go back if you want to, but I'm not coming with you. The guy was rude and creepy. I recommend you not to go back there either." Maggie said. She stared out the window. "His face was bruised with tons of cuts. His eyes were red, like death."

"Or exhaustion, or injuries." I whispered

"Don't be insensitive." She yelled.

"Ok, sorry." I listened as she talked and described him so vividly. She was distraught. She talked less and less after describing him, she cried. I tried my best to comfort her. As we arrived at the school dorms Maggie sat for a minute and said nothing.

"Let's look at other buildings for the class assignment. Especially if it's a chance he's going to keep going back there.

"Vicki is going to take care of that situation. We've been to different places and this is the most ideal one we've seen." I said.

"Gina no. we can find a building ten times better. I know you Gina. Stay away from that place. If you can't understand, we don't need to do this assignment together." She stormed out of the car, slamming the door so hard the window vibrated. I can't believe that guy made her uncomfortable that she'd give up being partners with me on this. I've known her for five years and she's a confident go getter. This man had her in shock. I met Maggie at seventeen, working at a convenient store, where I was a cashier and stocked. She was a manager and she would always talk at lunch breaks. We became close friends and now we're in college together.

Her fear of this guy, stirred up my own fears. I hated getting close to people. How it hurts to be with them instead of without them. When I was younger, I would always sit in a corner and sing. I had no close friends. I never wanted to get close to anyone, because if I did, they would always disappear. At eight, my first friend was Brian Walters. We did everything together; played with worms and dirt all the things kids do. We would pretend to go on adventures in abandoned places. Brian taught me how to pick the safety locks on doors. It was exciting to get from one place to our next destination. One day we were walking home from school and five boys picked on me. Brian hit one with a rock in the face, days later we found out the boy died. Brian ended up getting sent to a juvenile home, his family moved, and I never seen him again.

In the ninth grade I had a best friend named Korey Gooden. She loved to dress up and wear makeup. We'd always hang out at the malls and she introduced me to boys. One night, we both snuck to a party which became wild quick. Korey ended up being shot. She recovered and her family banned her and me from being friends. We had to avoid each other in school until my family and I moved. My dad and mom divorced when I turned sixteen. My father had problems with drinking and mom worked constantly and it angered him. It was always an issue. Sometimes they fight and I'd hide from the yelling and screaming. I haven't seen him for years. My mom always sent me to grandmas because she worked and then my grandmother whom I was grew close to, had died and I stopped trusting people a long time ago. They all would leave me. Maggie has been my only friend for all these years.

That night, I laid awake. The tension became too much in the dorm room. Maggie stumped around angry before going to bed. She refused to discuss the project, and slamming things down. It was extra annoying when she put on headphones to drown out the conversation I attempted to make with her. Every time she glanced at me she would turn her music louder and louder. Eventually she fell asleep, probably with the intentions of not speaking to me in the morning. I was curious of what Maggie saw, how one guy frighten her. I thought about having to search for another building for our class assignment, and thought about how much I wanted to fight her on this. The loving side of me understood and never would want anyone to make me do something I didn't want to. This day had been mind-boggling. So I turned out the lights and tried to force myself to go to sleep.

All my efforts of trying to sleep failed because I kept thinking about the blood Maggie described over the man's face. I would be hurt if they found his body in that building and I knew about him, but did nothing. But, the realtor said she would handle it. So why did this continue to bother me? I jumped out of bed, slipped on clothes, and snuck out of the dorm room. The building wasn't too far from the school, so I walked there. I remember Vicki telling us the side door was always open. So I knew how to get in. The gate was the problem.

I walked through the alley and to the gate with my flashlight. The chains were wrapped around tight. I looked around to see if there was something I could pick the locks with, but naturally there was nothing. "Damn! Now I have to climb the gate." This gate was tall and appeared like prison gates. I may be exaggerating a little bit, but it was huge. I hadn't realized how big they were the last time I was here. I examined from the ground, walking from side to side, I inhaled and exhaled before climbing. There were no space between the barbwire, I just began to climb. I threw my legs over one by one. My left side of my jeans snagged the wire. I gripped the fence with my left hand and tried to get my pants loose with the right. I cut the palm of my hand pulling hard, slipping off the gate. The cut on my hand was minor, but when I held my hand closed the blood dripped. It could've been worse than what it was, but thank God it wasn't. It's like grazing your arm against something and if my hand was positions any other way it could have been serious. It's was very painful. It took a minute to get up, and when I did I hopped all the way to the door, and went in. I pulled my small flashlight from my pocket and I shined it all over.

"Hello? Is anyone in here?" I yelled and the echo scared me. As I walked around I listened to the noise and I flashed the light toward the sound, but I saw nothing. "Why am I the stupid girl from the scary movie that searches for the trouble?" I made it to the front area. "Hello?" I said, but there was silence. I continued to move towards the front. Every step I took my heart raced. I was afraid of what I would see, hear or feel at this point.

"Why are you here?" A man said, and I screamed when I heard his voice. "What is your purpose?"

"I came here looking for you." I said holding my chest, watching the dark figure move as I moved flashing the light towards the sound of his voice.

"Why?" He said.

"My friend said you were hurt earlier, I wanted to know if you needed help."

"You're friend seen blood, but I'm still breathing as you can see." He was standing in the shadows across the room from me. His voice deep, but calmed and not at all harsh as it was earlier.

"Come into the light, I like to see the people I'm talking to." I said.

"I rather not, and I'm insisting you leave!" His tone was harsh and straight to the point.

"Why are you hiding from me?" I asked walking towards him. I saw him backing further into a corner.

"No need to overstep the boundaries that has been laid before you. My appearance should be the last of your concerns." He said moving deeper into the darkness.

"Why?" I asked

"I won't let you. You have been warned." He said.

"I have been warned... What do you mean I have been warned? I skipped, climbed, and fell trying to check to see if you were still breathing." I put my cut hand on my hip, and snapped it off, as he became invisible to my eyes.

"Enough with this combat conversation. Leave now!" He stepped towards the front a little where the shadow was dim, and I could make out his shape.

"I'm here to make sure you're not a corpse." I said.

"In your world this would be a naïve, dangerous situation, and you could become the corpse."

"Did you put me under a spell to make me come back to become a corpse?" He chuckled as he raised his arm and my vision became faint and I heard his voice say "Kliziora."

I jumped up looking at the clock and it was the next evening. I look around trying to figure things out. How did I get to my dorm room? How did he know where I live? Why did I pass out? My phone rang and I noticed on the caller i.d. it was Maggie. I didn't realize that there was a posted on my forehead. I pulled it off and read it. "Oh no!" I said I was late meeting Maggie at her job. Was that a dream? It was so weird. Why would I dream of a mysterious man? Maggie's words of this guy was permanently etched in my head, along with me seeing the shadow, it bothered me. I had so many questions but had so little answers. I drove to Maggie's job, but as I turned the corner I passed the building and at that moment it had to be more than a dream. This was real, I felt it. I don't know why the building bothered me the least. I wanted to bring it back up. It was time to beg Maggie to change her mind. I pulled up to Maggie's job as she stood waiting. She got into the car. "Where the hell were you, I've been calling your phone all day. Are you in the same clothes? " Maggie said examining me.

"I over slept. I don't understand how I slept so long, must be because I'm tired." I said. I noticed I was in the same clothes from yesterday.

"Gina since you are not working you should pick up my slack and go full force with this project when I'm at work." Maggie said. "Check out some other buildings."

"I know, speaking of the project, about that building..."

"No, Gina."

"Maggie, please! This is a great place, I'm sure the realtor had the cops get rid of the guy by now. We can take the pictures and leave." I begged.

"I said I don't want it. Why do you feel so strongly about this place? It will take thousands of dollars to make this building the way we want it." She snapped.

"Because, when I walked in there I could feel it in my gut that it is the right place. And it's going to get us an A."

"Gina!"

"Maggie!"

"Is it about the grade that keeps you so adamant about this place?" Maggie asked observing me for the answer.

"Yes Maggie, It's the grade we can earn." I pouted.

"I've been calling you and you've slept all day from your late night outing. I thought we would have time for dinner to discuss it and because you were still captivated by it. I made the call and made it happen. But you're going alone to get the pictures today got it?"

"Got it. Thank you, what made you change your mind?" I hugged her.

"I got your back Gina, and if you feel strongly that this is the place for us. I don't want to let you down."

"Thank you, thank you. You won't regret it." I clapped my hands excited.

"Yeah, yeah, yeah I know. Go! The appointment is in ten minutes. I'll leave you to it."

"Ten minutes when were you going to tell me Maggie." I asked.

"Now, its three blocks away. You'll make it." Maggie said in a tone as if she didn't appear worried and smiled. She got out of the car and ran inside her job. I started up the car and drove off. Maggie was right. The building was a few blocks away. By the time I got there, it was getting dark; it was so cold out, and it's the start of winter and the cold it kicks in fast. I walked up to the building and waited for Vicki to come and let me in to take the pictures for our project. It was cold; I rubbed my arms up and down while standing there. I looked into the sky it was night already. It became darker and darker by each second. Part of me wondered if the guy was still here. I was wondering if he would try and run us off again. I stood waiting about ten minutes and then I reached for my phone and realized it was in the car. It began to snow very heavy. I ran to the car, and tried to get in. I was so happy because I locked my keys in the car. There were two men standing behind me. I could not see them because of all the heavy snow fall.

"Do you need help lady?" one of the men asked. His face was cleaned shaved and one of his eyes looked closed. He was short, bald and bulky.

"No I'm fine, thank you." I said hoping they would go away.

"Why don't you walk with us, we'll get you out of the snow." The other man laughed. This guy scared me. He was muscular, he had no coat on, and he looked me up and down as his nose spread and sniffed the air. His hair was black and long. He was very tall with a cut on his chin. But there was something different about them.

"No thank you." I walked away, this was a bad situation.

"I was telling you, not asking you." The guy grabbed me. He stuck his tongue out and it resembled a snake's tongue. I screamed loud as I struggled to get away from the guys I turned and punched the short one as hard as I could. The other guy knocked me down, and I hit my head. Everything became blurry; I heard a noise, and after a few seconds, it felt like I was floating in thin air, I was too weak to fight. I blacked out.

When I regained consciousness, my head was pounding. I was trying to focus my eyes, and when they were clear, I wasn't at home. I tried to stand up but couldn't, I was soaking wet lying by a fire. I tried to get up once again. The room was so beautiful, bright, sheer thick curtains hung from the ceiling, with golden rods holding them up. The walls had stenciling on them in different colors. The floors were warm and I wondered why those two guys would bring me to a place like this? It was beautiful, and unlike any room I have ever seen in my life. There were beautiful colors I have never seen unless it was my eyes not focusing.

"Don't get up, you might hurt yourself." A male voice said.

"Where am I? Who are you?" I said and looked around for the face that matched the voice.

"That doesn't matter." The voice said.

"Where am I?" I asked.

"Somewhere you shouldn't be."

"If you're going to kill me at least show your face." I struggled, and I stood up.

"Kill you!" the voice chuckled. "If I hadn't been here you would've gotten killed."

"You're not one of those guys?" I felt myself shaking, I don't know if it's because I'm cold or frightened.

"No."

"Let me go if you're a good guy." I snapped.

"Good guy, I never said I was a good guy."

"Who are you? You are creeping me out." I said.

"I warned you never to come back here. Now you want to leave! Now you fear for your tomorrow, don't you?" The voice was heavy and escalated.

"What do you mean you warn me not to come back? I've never been here.... wait, the building." I said to myself. "You saved me!" I looked around and noticed the possibility I was in one room in the abandon building. "It was two of those men, how did you get rid of them?"

"You are dangerously persistent." He stepped out of the dark and revealed himself standing with his head and body covered by a cloak.

"Are you always so rude to people you meet?"

"I don't dwell among the people here!" He said.

"You are these people you don't dwell around, but I'm a little different, my name is…." I tried to get a good look at his face.

"Gina, I know!" He says as he grabbed wood on the side of the fireplace and tossed it into the fire. At the moment I felt some kind of fondness towards him when my name parted his lips. I couldn't see his hands just gloves. I couldn't figure out why he was covered up.

"So, do you have a name, super dude? Or do you want to remain anonymous?" I asked still looking around the cleanliness of the room and the beautiful antiques.

"Aden!" He said.

I walked towards him and extended my hand, "Nice to meet you."

"Wisely I can see it won't be." Aden backed away to leave his appearance mysterious.

"Well, can I at least see the man, who saved me?"

"I gave you no indication I wanted to be comrades with you or anyone else." Aden walked away. He went towards a dark corner on the opposite side of the room. "You can leave freely in the morning, until then, there's a bed lie down and keep to yourself."

"You are so rude...I'm leaving now." I walked towards the door. The door slammed.

"It's not safe." Aden held the door, "You can leave in the morning. These are my quarters, get rest, and keep to yourself."

"How did you do that?" I asked noticing how swiftly he moved from one side of the room towards the door.

"No need to talk, use this time to rest." Aden said. I walked towards the bed and sat down.

"Are you my personal superhero now?" I watched him go into the shadows and remained curious to see what he looked like. "Why are you in the dark?" I asked.

"I believe the proper way to say is that I prefer it that way."

"Is that cape just for costume, or do you prefer to stay hidden?" I asked.

"My cloak is for my personal solitude." He said. I tried all night to stay awake, but I couldn't fight the drowsiness. My eyes got heavier and heavier. I slept for a long time and I dreamed of Aden and oddly he revealed himself as a prince. When I opened my eyes, and I laid staring at the ceiling. I knew where I was and it wasn't a lavish place it was my dorm room. I sat up in the bed and looked around. "Aden!" I called out his name.

"No! Who in the world is Aden? You're lucky I have a key. I thought something happen to you yesterday," Maggie said handing me a cup of water.

"No! I just… I don't know. I feel weird."

"It looked like you bumped your head on something." She said dabbing my head with a cloth to clean it.

"Maybe you need to go to the hospital and get it checked out."

"Maggie, no, I'm fine."

"When the real estate lady called me and said she couldn't make it for our appointment, I called you and you never picked up." She stared at me. "I was worried. You've been going M.I.A on me Gina."

"I'm sorry, I know. I've been tired after trying to get this project finished and ready for class. I'm sleeping more that's it. I'm catching up on much needed rest." I replied.

"Gina give yourself an extra day. You're acting weird now. You sure you're okay?"

"I'm fine, promise."

I know that it's something bigger going on. This mystery had my attention. Am I hallucinating, or dreaming? I'm trying to figure out if Aden is a figment of my imagination, or if he is real. The thought of him saving me and being my very own superman elated me. I wanted nothing more, than to unmask him. I paced around all day in my room wondering, how did he get in here? I went looking for my car. It was outside, like it was never moved. Did he drive it here? It seemed like I never left the room. It angered me, because both times I awaken in my dorm room. Aden doesn't leave a note or a message or anything. I think I was becoming obsessive. "Gina. Gina!" Maggie yelled trying to snap me out of my trance.

"Yeah. I'm sorry did you say something?" I shook my head.

"Yes, you have to go meet the Realtor at the building… are you okay, you are totally bugging right now. She wants to meet with you again."

"The building, right let me put my shoes on. And I'll go."

"Wait? I'm going with you, because you seem to disappear when you go there."

"No, no, no!"

"What? Why?"

"You're scared remember, I can take the pictures, so you don't have to go there." I nudged her back.

"No, I'm not afraid. I can go. And I am going. Now let's go." She held her head up with certainty and walked straight out the door.

Maggie was driving and she was listening to her favorite cd. She had it blasting and we usually get into it about the crazy song, but today, it didn't bother me. "Ok, I know something's wrong. You hate this song!"

"It's cool. I'm just tired. No energy to talk, or argue." I avoided her eyes.

"Oh, she's here." Maggie said as we pulled up to the building. Vicki was standing waiting for us.

Maggie was the first to get out. I exhaled and then I followed. We walked up to the building; She and the Realtor were talking I was just anxious for the realtor to open the gates so that I could go in to find Aden. I wanted Maggie to see, that even though he was annoying, he was a good guy.

"Let's go in. You ladies don't have to worry; the man has not been back here. So you can take your pictures," The realtor said.

"You ready?" I asked Maggie.

"Yeah, I'll be fine."

We went in the building and walked around. We went through the rooms and took plenty of pictures. The place I was in when we first discovered this place wasn't even visible. Now I knew it was something wrong. It made me feel like I was hallucinating ever being inside of it. Did he leave? Did he ever exist? Did I actually go through the things my bruises show I went through last night? Am I having a mental breakdown? I would hate that I ran him away. In the front, I took pictures and as the real estate lady talked, I searched around.

"Ladies, it was nice working with you. I hope you get a good grade in your class. I also hope that this will be a fitting place for the Design Town Corporation." The realtor said.

"We hope so too, the teacher is tough when he's grading." Maggie said.

As I became bewildered at the possibility I maybe imagining the events of the last couple of days, I tried to stay involved with the discussion; "Yeah, like a professor he will tell you how he wants your work done once, and you have to go from there." I said as we began to exit the building. A weird vibe came over me and I glanced to the side and I saw Aden. He was leaning against a post that was wooden and carved with designs of leaves, but as soon as I blinked he was gone again. Vicki closed the door I shook my head with confusion. I had full determination later on, to bring my eyes, my mind, and my heart into one union.

Chapter 2: The First Encounter

I sat and reminisce about my father as I always do as I watched this ever ambitions Gina leave with her friends. It reminded me of his ambition in many conversations we had. I remember all the things he had done for me. The last conversation we had sticks out in my mind every day, because this was the last time I saw him, and the image of his face, the structure of his body, and the story that he revealed to me. One day, we sat in an Urn room full of falling family affiliates. The Urns were decorated according to class; Rubies for leaders, Emeralds for soldiers, Crystals for adolescent, but the Onyx, the big black Onyx stone was for Kings, who ruled every war. The walls were painted with drawings of soldiers, and creatures that fought hard and long days of certain combats. The floors were thick with gold and shapes unknown to my eyes. I was an immature boy, I endured a lot, but I remember my father words.

"Aden, my son... do you see that your skin differs from mine?" my father asked.

"Yes father! Why is that?"

"I am what they call a full blooded Fira. Your mother was half Phantom blood and human blood."

"Do I resemble her father?"

"You do my son. For years I have told you stories about my childhood, and how I had to protect you from things. My time has come, so I must explain to you things you will face while I'm gone."

"When you are gone? Father what are you talking about?"

"There was a war one-hundred years ago, between beasts, creatures and phantoms."

"You said there were no wars. That our country had been with peace, from your father days of war." I said. He held up his hand to shush me. So I sat in silence as he spoke.

"There was nothing but slashing of swords, heavy breathing, blood and one beast after another in a dark civilization. If you were a person coming into this realm off the Nitzers, the traveling tanks you have grown fond of Aden, you would swear this war could have been between our whole universe. This war began between Fira, Phantoms and She-ads. Firas are live fire beasts; we have the strength of a thousand armies. We unite the countries together and everyone knows there's nothing to fear. The fire we use is energy from our people. If the leader, which is I were to die the Firas lose half of their power until they agree to elect another. They could perish as well if they never agree on a new king. I hold enough power that if I burst into flames I could take out this world, and maybe others around us. No one dares to step out of line with the Firas, with me as their leader. This world was created by a light source that dwelt inside our universe for eras. We call this source Mother Light. We also show our gratitude to its rise and fall throughout the days."

"Please father, continue because I cannot understand." I said as my mind raced to put things together.

"There is this myth in our world, which says billions of eras before us an explosion created our world and the surrounding worlds. Fragments from this explosion was buried underneath the sands on the deserted planet we now call Earth. Eras after that when Being kind arrived A scientist named Ivon Re discovered this tiny specimen while researching on a continent. He took this fragmented item and stuck it into a cube. He stored it in to a cooling area and spent countless days trying to figure out its origin. A year later Ivon came across this study, it showed the extracted material pieces were created from dust particles that had been floating in the universe for billions of eras. It crashed through the Earth's atmosphere. Ivon noticed the twenty-third of December the cube floated and had turned into a stone. With one touch, a grasp from Ivons hand the stone exploded with light. Different beams of fragment were released piercing each of the eight Beings that were located in the room. When they opened their eyes they were here on Nexima. They thought the stone spoke out, but still to this day they don't know where the voice came from. It spoke out these words, "To here you were sent, the planet Nexima. A new life has been placed upon you to recreate a world that has been defiled with travesty. You are now a new breed; Fira, Phantom, Skin, She-ad, Spolra(Speed demon), Zentravepez, Foldinam, Lenzanad (Mixbreed), and Diminutive.""

"What am I to do with it?" I asked as my father handed me the Onyx stone. I looked at him afraid of what he would say.

"It will lead you and shelter you in the times of trouble. Each heir to the throne has one, except we keep them from the Grivens. They cannot handle such power. Each breed created, Phantoms are spirits, the closest to human beings. Their intelligence are higher, and have the most ability to use rituals without negative effects. They are their own version of Gods created amongst their land. Phantoms have the powers to float, glide, speed, and cast a ritual so detrimental you could suffer in agony, but the rituals are to be used for protection. She-ads are creatures who shed innocent blood and who intentionally kill. But the deaths they bring are far worse than guns and swords, its fear itself. Skins are closer to Beings able to reproduce constantly and mate with all our kind. Their only power is to make things appear. Spolra are demons who are fast and have the ability to stretch their limbs. Their claws are damaging and they move like four legged beasts. These creatures weigh two-hundred to four-hundred pounds each. Zentravepez are a female breed. They reproduce only female species and can control the male species of all kinds with sexual emotion giving off a certain scent. Their power varies. Foldinams are protectors of our planet. Guards of our kings. They become elders, and are two legged and four armed beasts depending on the mixtures. Lenzanad are warriors of our Advisors, and Elders, no one knows their abilities, and it is wise to stay away from them. And the Diminutive are our scientist, full of knowledge and more." My father said.

"How did the war begin?" I asked.

"It began when creatures, beasts, and spirits refused to give away what belong to them, our land, our homes, and our lives." My father said.

"Why do they kill?" I asked.

"The She-ads feel they are superior towards any worlds that live amongst the universe. If anyone infiltrates their way of living or thinking, they kill. The She-ads take their knowledge and their possessions and spread it through their society. Everyone and everything else is insignificant.

"If you're live fire and mother is a spirit, how did I come to be?"

"There are what they call, mating rituals. We were never to use them unless with our own kind. Your mother and I fell in love. The Firas and Phantoms were never enemies; they worked together on everything, except cross breeding.

"So, I am not to be here?" I asked.

"No, you were planned. You see the prophecy that everyone knew, but I. That a son with human Skin, Fire and Phantoms spirit would be born and rid the world of She-ads."

"Father," I said because I did not understand "How can a Phantom have flesh inside their blood?"

"There is a world called Earth, where many human Skins, that we call Beings dwell. They live in an atmosphere where they are free. That's where your mother migrated from with her parents." My father said.

"Her parents were Beings?"

"No, Aden. Spirits live inside Beings. It's their source of knowledge, and emotions. Her father was full of this, but her mother was from our world and was a Skin, could possibly resemble Beings. Skins are flesh on the outside, but survive from the use of their brain and heart but there was something different."

"What's different?" I was intrigued.

"She's full of power, speed, and rituals." He said.

"So mom came to be by mating rituals?"

"Yes. But not by our worlds mating rituals. You will learn when you're older, I'm sure." He chuckled.

"What about the prophecy that made me?" I asked.

"That a son with human Skin, live fire and Phantoms spirit was to be born and rid the world of She-ads. Your mother knew this. She was the chosen female of her civilization to bare the phenomenon child.

She was to choose from all the Firas and I was the chosen one. I was not to know of this, but your mother told me right before you were born."

"How can I be this champion?"

"Because no one knows your abilities. You can do things none of us can do."

"Father, I'm not ready for this responsibility. Not now."

"It is now 1909 my son, what you have become at the era of fifteen, you can do many things. This is important for you to know because you are the first of your kind. I will soon be destroyed. You can never die, unless the one who holds the power of the She-ads slay you. That's why you should kill him first."

"Father, what are you saying?"

"You are a Firatom Aden, which means, the only one. You are special! After my death you will no longer be able to touch anyone that is not of our kind, the powers that you have are to protect yourself. Promise me one thing." His words became faint.

"Anything father." I grabbed his hand.

"Marry Nirew. Marry her not just for love, but for the sake of our land and people."

"Father, are you okay." I asked. Seconds later a huge creature entered through the walls, with a disfigured body, no eyes, and hands bigger than elephant's feet. I watched it attack my father. He was angry and told me to run but I didn't listen. A burst of light and he turned into a huge ball of flames. His anger consumed him and he fought to the death. He was murdered, and his body returned to its normal form, and when I touched him he caught fire. This thing could smell my presence. His nose sniffed and his hand reached for me, so I ran, so fast so far away from the creature. I dwelled hidden in Nexima lower valleys for eras. No one knew where I was. I would travel and there were rumors that I was in one village or another, but no one really knew.

As a boy I learned to find food, shelter and how to take care of myself as part of my training. My father would take me far out and leave me to fend for myself. I always succeeded. It is different now I couldn't blend in, it didn't work everyone knew I was out of place. My clothing was not of their kind. I tried to make them dirtier, but it still didn't work. So I would bounce back and forth to other villages. It became frustrating when my father's guards and advisors started to search the villages for me. I covered myself with my black cloak that my father had given me when I was thirteen eras.

I had grown six feet. This cloak kept me hidden from all and this is how I migrated around without being noticed. I watched how different villages worked hard and the little scraps they had left at the end of the sunset they would get stolen by village guards. Their kings were heartless. There were countless of starving children. I eventually began to get angry. I had to do something. I fought making it known that no one was to take from these villages again. I wanted to get away from the responsibility. I wanted to leave Nexima all together. The constant reminders of my father's death tortured me. I searched for my father's killer. She-ads attacked me. I traveled further into hiding. I pulled out the Onyx stone my father gave me one night; I rubbed it and closed my eyes. When I opened my eyes, I didn't recognize my location. It was strange this place was full of Skins walking around. There were transporting devices moving fast through this large gray path I stood in the middle of. "Move it. Get out the street." A male specie yelled. I move back. I grew up by myself and the She-ads followed me to this strange place. It's was a battle. I constantly fought them, but I couldn't figure out how to defeat them, because they never let me touch them. It was a struggle to take them all on. Most days it was two at a time, and other days it was four or five. I was thankful my father trained me a little before his passing. I left my world in 1954, and lived amongst the Beings. I was never to compare them to the Skins in my world, because it was like disrespect to them, they feel as though Beings are lesser than they. This is where I met a man named Suecko. I found his name on a pole outside of a building. He gave me shelter and food to eat. He knew I would be arriving.

"You have a destiny that's bigger than you know." Suecko said.

"What do you mean?" He looked so convinced.

"You are one-hundred and thirty-seven in your world, but here you look no older than a nineteen year old boy. You are from far away and God has sent you to save lives."

"I am not here to save lives. I'm here searching for someone." I said.

"Someone you hate, I sense it." He said.

"This one, he killed my father." If I said creature, it would cause pandemonium in this world. No one here was used to seeing what I saw my whole life.

"I can train you. It's my job. God has chosen me to help you on your journey." Suecko said.

"Look, thanks for lending me your home for these few months. I think I need to go." I got up from the floor and walked away and he was right in front of me. "You were sitting, how did you do that?"

"I glide like your mother."

"You know nothing about her." I yelled.

"I told you I have been chosen. Do you feel its coincidence you ended up here?"

"I don't want to train; I want to kill the bastard that killed my father." I said

"Searching with vengeance and hate in your heart will get you killed first."

"Get out of my way." I tried to push him but his movement was quick. This made me so angry then. I swung and went at him with everything I had, but I couldn't touch him.

"Fighting with anger will get you killed. You can't concentrate on what you're doing. The creature you are to face will rip you to shreds. You are the last of your family, but you must preserve yourself because you are one of your species. You can be the best if you let me help you Aden."

I didn't understand how he knew so much. In the three months I had been with him, I spoke nothing. Not a word. I put my ego aside and trained with him. We didn't just train physically, it was mentally as well. He told me my father had visited him a month before he had died, and warned him I would come to this world in case of his death. Suecko was to be aware and be vigilant to the skies. I became equipped with skills in street fighting, boxing, and martial arts. I learned a lot of rituals and studied hard to understand my world and culture of this world. I am also trained to use every weapon you can imagine. Suecko always preached to find ways to open my heart about certain things. He was like a second father to me. A short while after, he died of a heart attack. Before he passed he told me, I had learned well, and I will serve my purpose. He told me that I would find what will make me young sooner than I thought. I ventured out into this world alone. Not knowing much, but quickly picked up the routines of the streets. I knew how to co-exist without being noticed at all. These strange creatures on Earth was different and difficult to maneuver around. The air was exhausting to inhale, seem thick and I couldn't adjust to it. For the first time in my life I felt sick and couldn't get acclimated with the speed these Beings used, which was not fast at all. They moved so slowly. They walked not glide. They ran not flown. It was different, but peaceful to not have to be in a hurry all the time. But, this made me lazy. I would walk on the street and the mocking of my cloak came from these insolent male species. I realized I looked about their age, but honestly I was eras older. So once again, I seek shelter. Hiding again was something I did not want to do. I overheard a conversation about a place that was not in use. I went to its location and tried to open the handled and it broke off. I walked in. Everything was always locked. This place was dark and dirty, but I had finally figured the stone out. I read the inscription on it and a light shined. I thought of my favorite place, and it appeared. It was my quarters in Nexima, it was an exact duplicate. I walked to the door because I heard something, I opened it and my home was here. I slammed the door. Why would it bring me back to Nexima. But I noticed it was others doors as well, I opened them all, and they all lead to different places. How could this be? I didn't understand this stone as well as I hoped I did. This was of a power I didn't understand, but if I talked to people who did, I would know. She-ads tracked me down. They became very outlandish with the Beings at night. The Beings never knew they would lose their lives to things that never existed in their world. The fights with the She-ads became easier as I fought them. I searched for them and whenever they came my way, I kill them. Now I'm older I'm slowing down because I've been on Earth so long. My body is not tolerable to Earth's oxygen, and I've been trying to find things to keep me in shape. Beings have a limited life span as of in my world I can dwell the longest existence possible. My father had never told me what he did to stay healthy for three-hundred years. He always said it was one thing that kept him young and that I would discover it as I became older. He had spoken similar words as Suecko. I began wondering because whatever it was I needed it soon.

    After my run in with those college girls I went hunting, as I often do. The She-ads were good at disguising themselves as Beings and going on killing sprees. These creatures wait until people are walking down the streets or sometimes jump in front of cars. The She-ads have no eyes, but they have a heighten sense of smell. They know the height and weight of their victim before attacking. When devouring their victim it's like a drug, they can't stop, and kill again and again. Eventually they take on too much and die. If the She-ads were lucky most nights they would survive. I found two in the alley behind the building I settled in. I crept up to them, and they realized my presence. I decided to cater to their egos before I laid them to rest. As I approached one of the She-ads spoke. "I know that smell from anywhere..." it sniffed the air turning towards me "The presence of good with a hint of darkness. They say the worst half-breed you'll ever come across. Is this your attempt to diminish our race, like your fathers? You will never destroy us, we will never go away." It whispered.

"Like an old Beings saying, try until you succeed." I said attacking them with my sword I pulled from my waist. Two more She-ads grab me from behind and held me down.

"Your father couldn't kill us, and neither can you." It punched me in the face and I kicked him off me, throwing the other two across the alley.

"Maybe not, but it pleasures me to finish what he started." I said as we circled, I was watching my back

"Aden! The hero! The one who's supposed to destroy us. You'll never make it past me." The She-ad ran towards me, he ran into my sword.

"That's enough talking." Two more She-ads approached. I threw them to the ground with all the strength I had. They weighed at least two-hundred pounds each, some even more. I was slashed on the chest as more creatures approached and I fought them. It was like being surrounded in a bad nightmare, but I killed because I knew I had to. If I didn't kill them, they certainly would kill me. I was weakening after every fight. It's like I had nothing to live for. At every battle I would fight like it was my last. I fought hoping that one would kill me. Hoping it was the end. I'm hoping to meet the one who can defeat me. I couldn't stand living without my father all these eras and the more I fought I wanted to see him. I will not give up during a fight. My father would never accept failure. He never liked for me to give up on anything. After that battle, I took off my gloves and touched every She-ad I fought. I couldn't leave bodies lying around, especially those of things never seen in this world. As I weakly staggered back I entered the building only to find Gina was just sitting waiting. I stepped in a dark part of the room and stayed there.

"I told you to stay away." I said.

"I thought you left here." She responded jumping to her feet at the sound of my voice.

"Maybe I should have." I had to lean against the wall to conceal the bleeding. I knew she would care for my injuries.

"I don't know why I'm here. I'm just curious I guess. How do you survive? How do you eat?" Gina asked.

"More questions!" I snapped.

"What's that supposed to mean?" she asked.

"You will always have more questions to ask me. It's best if you don't concern yourself with my existence."

"Well I'm a one-hundred and one question person; let's go for two-hundred shall we." She said so sarcastically scrubbing the floor with her shoe.

"Let's don't and say we did."

"Are you this cranky all the time?"

"Cranky? Unlikely, annoyed maybe." I felt myself slipping and I was going to fall.

"I searched for the room. What happened to that room Aden?" Gina asked.

"Gina, its late go home. The more you indulge yourself with my existence, you're not better off." I cupped my chest as the blood was forming around my hand.

"What did you do Aden?" Gina asked as she looked at me losing my balance. I grunted and fell to the floor as I always do when I'm hurt after a battle. It takes a whole night for me to heal. The pain this time was excruciating. There was little darkness in the room. I fell into the light. I tried to pull myself up so she couldn't see me.

"Aden, are you okay?" She ran towards me.

"No! Don't touch me. Please!" I yelled and she stood still.

"Why can't I move?"

"Don't come near me."

"Why?"

"Stay there." I said. I was taught rituals by Suecko in our world, if anyone or you were endangered, to keep them out of harm you make them immobile. The more they struggle to get free, the stronger the rituals hold will be. I had to use it. Touching her was not in the plan. I didn't want to hurt her. "You can't touch me." I dimmed the lights as quickly as possible, and left the room.

"Aden?" she said.

When I released Gina the lights brighten, and she repeated my name. I went somewhere that she could not follow. I stood against the wall, as I smelt her scent walking pass. I don't know how this will work with her being here every day. If the She-ads know she's here they will kill her to get to me. Even though she had no meaning to me, I still didn't want her getting hurt. I couldn't be responsible for an accidental death. This night was going to be a long one. The pain went through my skin like a power surge. The cut across my chest turned green, and bubbled. I yelled snatching the cloak off me, and I dropped to the ground. It sizzled as if I was burning. The flesh was healing itself, tugging and pulling back together. This part is much worse than the cuts and bruises.

I awakened early daybreak. I smelled Gina. She was still here. I walked around to find that she was asleep on the floor. She slept against the wall and looked at peace. She was worried, that's why she didn't leave. I had half a mind to let her stay, but she needed to be home. Still I didn't bother her. So I watched. I was getting an unusual need to see her. I didn't want to leave. So I sat down beside her. It was something drawing me in. I wanted to touch her face, and she turned over. I wanted to snap out of this yearning, and quickly move, but I couldn't. She opened her eyes, and I turned my head.

"How long have you been sitting there?" She asked as she awakened a little groggy.

"Not long. I just sat here." I stood up with my head turned from her.

"You don't have to leave." She said.

"its daybreak, it's safe for you to leave."

"Are you okay, I seen the blood on the floor." Gina asked.

"I'm fine! I took care of my wounds."

"You didn't look like it, do you need some help?" She was so sympathetic.

"You shouldn't have been here!" I snapped.

"Wow, you are such a grouch."

"I'm fine. I took care of the blood."

"How, I didn't see you leave to go to the hospital."

"I took care of it my way. It's time to go home now."

"Fine, Aden! Hopefully you find someone else to be as gracious to you as I've been." She stormed out of the building. I was curious of why she's so drawn to this place? Why is there a need for me to see her? It was bothering me. I had a moment of great agony and I kicked the crate next to me on the floor.

I couldn't understand this moment and I laid and fell into a deep trance. It felt like a dream of my father, but it was all too real. He stood with a shine of diamond dust around him. His complexion was gray, with no color.

"My son, your energy, and your youth will be restored sooner than you think." My father said.

"How father? I'm always so weak. It's plenty of them, and one of me." I said

"Aden, you have to open your mind and your spirit. Meditate! You will see." He said.

"Father, I need you to tell me. I can't do this much longer." I said.

"You are stronger than this Aden."

"I will be joining you soon if you don't help me damn it." I yelled. My father just stared and shook his head and faded away in the distant. I opened my eyes to the sound of a pat on the wall. It's that scent that's been lingering around a lot. I walked out to see what was going on.

"Why are you here again?" I said. She turned to look for me, but I stood far-off.

"Geez, do you always scare people like this?"

"You wouldn't be scared if you didn't come here." I paused and hesitated, "You shouldn't be here."

"Why?" She asked.

"It's trouble being around me, that's why? Did you ever leave?"

Gina giggled, "No, I walked around a while. I called my friend to pick me up. Anyway, the only problem I see is you sneaking around and scaring people, and taking me home. How do you get in any way? There's no sign of forced entry."

"I'm someone with many qualities." I said.

"Yeah, I've noticed Aden. Why won't you let me see you? Can't I at least see the man that's torturing me?"

"I didn't ask you to come here. I'm not torturing you, you can always leave." I became angry at her persistence.

"Calm down. I know I'm being bothersome. Don't blow your lid. I wanted to apologize for invading your space."

"So you're conscious of your stubbornness? Why don't you go home?" I tried not to be affectionate towards her at all.

"No more conscious of it than you are of yours. I don't want to leave, I like this place. It's very peaceful." She glanced around at a creaking sound. I looked around. I wondered, and my gut feeling was telling me it was She-ads. I keep it dark in here. Gina had opened the old curtains to let light in. But in an instance the creaking sound was from an old chandelier falling from the ceiling, I glided across the floor as Phantoms does and moved her quickly and she screamed from her flesh burning when I touched her. I circled the room very rapidly, I could see the way Gina had looked at me, her heart was racing, her mouth hung open, and her eyes stuck out, with drooping eyebrows with a pause of a still picture. After I knew she was safe from the falling chandelier, I smelled She-ads.

"Go home Gina, this is what I meant. You will get killed being so damn stubborn." I whispered, observing the possibilities of where the She-ads we're going to come from.

"I thought it wasn't safe for me out there." She said.

"It is daybreak. You'll manage well. It's not safe for you here right now. Go!" I couldn't understand why they were out during the daytime. They never take full form in the daytime. I heard a car pull up.

"Maggie is coming to get me. She's pulling up now. Go away so she won't see you!" Gina said "And thanks again. I owe you."

"If you leave we will be even." I said a She-ad jumped from the ceiling in front of Gina. She screamed.

"Run Gina." I yelled.

Maggie entered and out of nowhere she was knocked down by another She-ad. I killed as many as I could as they grew in number within the building. I watched them try to get away luckily stumbling at every attempt the She-ads made to grab them, but they were separated. Gina was thrown against the wall, I tried to get to her, but she was unconscious. I fought and killed one after another. There was one She-ad left, and it took its knife and shoved it straight into Maggie. "No." I yelled and glided over and killed the She-ad. Gina was alert now, and she seen Maggie on the ground covered in blood.

"Maggie. No, Maggie." She ran to her, and held her in her arms. "Maggie wake up. Maggie come on get up sweetie." She saw the blood all over her. "Maggie!" She screamed.

"She's gone. You have to go with me now." I called out to her.

"No! Maggie." She cried.

"Let's go or you will be next." I yelled.

"She needs help, I'm not leaving her." She yelled staring at me.

"Gina, your life depends on getting out of here." I yelled as Gina continued to cry holding her friends body. Half of mind wanted me to let her grieve and fiend for herself, but something else was telling me to take her with me.

"Gina I can't touch you, they're more of those things coming, come on." I yelled.

"Get us out of here. Get us somewhere safe. Please!" She asked holding Maggie. I glanced at them both, and I walked to Gina and touched her shoulder, steam rose from my hand and they both faded away. I noticed how much pain Gina was in. The hurt in her eyes looking as I looked at the empty space on the floor still cover with blood. The same face I had when I lost my father. Gina had stumbled into a new world and she didn't know it yet.

Chapter 3: The Whole Truth

All I could remember was being dizzy in front of the emergency doors, and the loud sound of the sidewalk cracking with Maggie lying in my arms. I screamed for help and doctors ran towards us with a stretcher. I watched them take her through the doors and they began, yelling at me asking me questions.

"Ma'am what happened?" A doctor asked. "What is her name?"

"Maggie, She was stabbed, please help her." I cried.

"We will need you to wait here."

"She's my friend I need to be with her." I cried as nurses held me back. I waited for almost two hours to see her. I walked back and forth in the hallway. I couldn't figure out what was going on. My mind was all over the place. Even though I worried, I felt safe, the hallway was warm. I sat on the floor watching patients being wheeled in and out of rooms. I still had no fear because Maggie was safe. When I walked into her hospital room, she laid lifeless. I wonder what she was feeling, if there's any pain. Did she hate me right now? The police officers came and asked a lot of questions I couldn't answer. I didn't know what was going on; I couldn't remember the event that happened that day. I stared out of the rooms' window. Hoping she would wake up. The officers wanted to take me to the station to continue to question me as if I was a suspect, but the interrogation stopped. I didn't know why, but I didn't care.

"She won't be awake for a while go home and get rest." A nurse said.

"I will soon. Thank you." I said as the nurse left the room. The room became warmer once again. I looked around. It's like we weren't alone. I felt protected in a way. I glanced at Maggie; I walked over to her, kissed her forehead, and walked out of the door. I caught a cab back to the dorm room and showered. When I returned to my room, it was dark. I reached for the lamp switching the light on. I looked around for a second. Usually it's pure laughter filling this space, and now it was dead silence. I cried just starring at Maggie's bed. For some reason it felt very gloomy, even with the lamp on. The window flew open, and a big gust of wind came through. I ran to the window and shut it. I felt creeped out. Those things I saw, I wonder what they were. I was angry at myself right now. Maggie alarm clock went off, and it jogged my thoughts clear. I tried to shut it off. I repeatedly pushed every button, but it wouldn't shut off, Finally, I got upset and I grabbed the alarm clock, snatched it from the wall and threw it across the room, and my tears would not stop falling. The alarm clock was tossed back on the bed.

"That's a healthy way to deal with your anger."

"Who's there?"

"Your friend, she's fine isn't she?" a deep voice came from the corner of the room. He stood from a stool and moving forward revealing a little bit of himself.

"Damn it Aden. Don't scare me like that," I quickly wiped the tears from my face. "How long have you been there?"

"I've been sitting here for a moment." Aden said.

"Are you trying to give me a heart attack?"

"No, but you will have one if you don't calm down. Your heart is racing a million miles per second."

"How do you know what my heart is doing?" I asked

"I observe a lot." Aden said.

"Were you at the hospital too?"

"What would make you ask that?" He responded.

"You give off a warm presence, and you make me feel protected. Just like I did coming into this room."

"How do you know this presence you speak of is me?" Aden asked.

"I feel the room getting warm when I'm around you. I can sense when you focus on me." I nervously grabbed my brush and brushed my hair.

"So do you feel protected?" Aden asked, and I didn't respond, but he kept talking, "She's okay, why are you still crying?"

"I'm upset. My best friend is in the hospital because of me being curious about a guy that she warned me to stay away from." I said. Aden said nothing. He stood eclipsed in the dark corner of the room.

The only thing visible on him was his lips. I day dreamed a moment about them. They were small, pink, and thin, for a minute they looked very inviting. At this moment I could imagine how attractive the face was attached to them.

"What's on your mind?" he asked. My thoughts were interrupted shifting into the next gear. "What were those things?" I turned from him, shaking the tension, the thoughts were steering my body.

"I told you it wasn't safe being around me."

"You told me, she told me, and I knew it." I said.

"So, why did you keep coming around?" He asked.

"I thought you could use a friend."

"I told you, I don't ..."

"I told you so's, will not make things better right now!"

"What will, I didn't ask you to come around and the fact that your friend is hospitalized in that bed is your fault not mine."

"Do you think I need you to tell me that?" I yelled.

"What do you want me to tell you then?" Aden became a little aggravated I could tell because his voice elevated so deep it echoed off the walls in the room.

"Tell me the truth. What's going on?"

"These creatures are called she-ads. Not human. They are not of this world."

"Aden, what do you mean not of this world?" I clenched myself to my bed waiting to hear more.

"It's a planet far away from here that can't even be seen by your NASA called Nexima. Many of my people don't exist anymore. It's now populated by She-ads and other Sawdawa species."

"What are you? You are human, right?" I asked. I couldn't believe those words had to actually come from my mouth. Was this why he was disguised all this time?

"I'm sure you know that I'm not human. I am from a race of three kinds of Sawdawa species. Live fire, Phantom, and Skins."

"Live fire! Is that why I was burnt when you touched me?" I rubbed my shoulder and my waist from the marks that were left earlier.

"Yes."

"Is that why you hide yourself?"

"No, Maggie situation is why I keep to myself, so when you humans see a guy walking with a cloak, the right sense would be to stay away.. But you... The She-ads are a ravaging race....! They have been after me for eras. They didn't want you or your friend."

"Eras? How old are you?"

"I'm a lot older than I look."

"Well, you haven't allowed me to see you yet, so you would have to tell me."

"Old!" Aden said.

"Are we talking twenties, thirties, or forties?"

"Gina, we have to leave here."

"What do you mean, we? Who exactly are you talking about?" I asked.

"You and I."

"No, I'm not going anywhere with you. You said it wasn't safe being around you. And judging by the situation, you were right." I stood from the bed and backed into a corner afraid of his next move.

"Now you have to because they will keep looking until they find you and kill you looking for me."

"Aden no, I'm not leaving Maggie. She's the only family I have. They will kill her." I said.

"Gina they think Maggie's dead by now. They pierced her with a poisonous sapphire blade."

"The doctor's said she was making improvements, and now you're telling me she will die." I yelled.

"One reason why I'm here is because there is not a surgery on your planet that can stop what's happening to her body right now. They don't know she is sick yet, but they will discover it, and it's going to kill her." Aden said.

"You don't know that. Maybe they can cure it whatever it is."

"This is not an earth illness she's dealing with. The reality of the situation is I'm from another time and another world and so are these things. They can't help her" Aden said.

"Then tell me what can, I refuse to let her die. Not when I'm not around." I felt the tears running down my face.

"What are you going to do? Sit here, cry, and pray she makes it through. I can help her, but I need your help to do it." Aden said.

"What do you need me to do, put my life and hers in the hands of a person who's been running away from these things for years?"

"I'm not running from anything. From my knowledge a stream in our forests sprouts a certain flower cup and blended with all the right ingredients it is said to help for this specific poison. But to help her you have to stay alive to get this remedy so you can bring it back to her. The people there at that facility can prepare the antidote." Aden said.

"I thought you were the last of your kind?"

"No I'm the last of my species, but the villagers with this remedy, they all are my kind. We have to go now. Every second we sit here and debate, her life is slipping away... Trust me! Let's go." Aden walked out of the room, and down the hall. It was like a strange movie, there were no signs of anyone. All doors were closed and as he walked all the lights flickered. He has a cool strut that makes your head bobble watching him. If you put him and a lot of guys in a cape and make them walk, you could identify him out of the bunch.

"How are we getting to this place?" I asked as we walked to an alley next to the dorm.

"You have been in an automobile before, haven't you?" He said as lights to a black car shined from a distance.

"You drive?" I said getting in this strange looking black car.

"It is best don't you think? I don't know if people would take too kindly to a guy flying in a black cape... would you?" He gave a smirk. "They would have him killed and analyzed. This whole world would be chaotic."

I had reasons not to trust him, but even more reason to trust him. Aden had saved my life more than once. He had gotten Maggie to the hospital quicker than I could've ever driven. He holds the key to the only way that Maggie and I will attend a movie again, or talk. I was terrified of being with him, but more petrified without him. My life has changed big time, just knowing that there is another world out there that no one knows about, or people know and is so caught up in the business of it, not caring of the other life on earth. I watched Aden from the side as we drove. I looked around at the accessories in the car, there's no radio, but there was a rectangular box with buttons. The car was silent. It's like a hummer, but more curvy like a corvette. I said nothing, but I notice a rock hit the car, and bounced off like something bouncing from a balloon. The inside material looked like a red wood grain dashboard.

Everything was silk when you touched it. The feeling of everything was thick, and cushioned. I looked up at the roof inside. I couldn't believe it, everything was beautiful porcelain made in the interior. The seatbelt holders were gold, and the hook that held it sparkled. The armrest sparkled with diamonds. I looked close, and there were actual diamonds. Who would have money to do this to their car? We traveled for two days and through our travels we stopped at hotels and rest stops so I could clean up. I noticed that he never ate or showered. He gave me utter privacy. I wondered why he had no odor, and why he wasn't hungry. But he gave money like it was an unlimited supply. I guess he really had his own way of doing things. He drove continuously non-stop, getting us to the closest rest stop on our journey to Sawdawa, he claimed. I noticed we came to an abrupt stop. This jerked my body. He made a turn and traveled about a mile, slammed on the breaks at an abandon church.

"What's going on?" I asked.

"I'm parking the car." He said.

"You're parking it out in the open like this?"

"It does seem like it's out in the open. Hold on." He said driving backwards busting through the fence of the vacant church. The car gained momentum, and it seemed he was aiming for the church.

"Uh, yeah… It's a building right there Aden! What are you doing" I screamed. I thought it was a bad time for him to kill himself. "Aden!" I covered my eyes, trying to breathe, but I paced my breath like a pregnant woman on tv in labor. I opened my eyes looking as we flew backwards. A light shined so bright that it blinded me. I closed my eyes tightly. When I opened my eyes again, we were inside the building. I had no broken bones, and there were no damaged to the car, nothing.

"Are you freaking crazy?" I yelled getting out of the car stepping into the abandon church, the lights were on. "Yeah…, let me answer for you. You are crazy." I slammed the car door looking around the church. I had never seen one that the inside looks like an enchanted castle. The ceilings were high; the colors were bright with greens, oranges, lavenders and porcelain everywhere.

"Calm down, you're perfectly fine." Aden's lips revealed a smirk. "It's not a car."

"Why the hell are you so calm? We could've died." His smirking was cute and aggravating. It was a turn on as well as a turn off. "What is it?"

"In human dialect it's a spaceship."

"Aden, you made it." I turned my head to see a tall, four-legged creature, purple with long green flowing hair that touched the back of her legs. She had four arms and a gold crown on top of her head, but besides that I was completely freaked out. I knew that I couldn't touch Aden, but I stood behind him, shielding myself.

"Queen Patano thanks again for your help." He said bowing to her.

"And she. This is the Being in search of a cure for her friend." Queen Patano said

"Yes." Aden motioned to me to bow, but I refused.

"Bow before me Being." Queen Patano snapped.

"I bow to no one, but God." I said.

"Gina, don't!" Aden turned to me with a surprise look, revealing a little more of himself to me.

"Where is your God? Who is your God?" She asked.

"Beings worship many God's My Queen." Aden snapped.

"She is in my presents, she must acknowledge me." She said.

"Just bow Gina." Aden whispered to me.

"No! I will not compromise who I am."

"Fool!" Queen Patano yelled looking irritated for a moment, as if she was trying to figure me out.

"Basauras!" Seconds after she yelled this name the floor shook for a moment before a creature appeared.

"My Queen." He said as if he were remorseful. "Damn it! This is our custom; you've been rude more than once just bow. Now." Aden yelled.

"I stand strong with God, and I will only bow to him. Not a man, nor a creature." I stood petrified, by what I seen, but I wouldn't compromise my morals, surely she could understand that. The creature breathed heavily. Aden stood in front of me.

"This won't be necessary." Aden said.

"Attack." Queen Patano spoke in a light voice. The creature yelled and ran towards Aden and I. Aden lifted his leg and kicked the creature backwards and it flew into a wall. Basauras stood shaking his head as the concrete bricks crumbled from the imprint of his body. He ran towards Aden and I screamed. He took Aden by the throat yelling at him as he rose him from the floor.

"Let him go please." I begged as I stood looking at Queen Patano whom looked well pleased at what she was seeing. Aden held the creatures' hands and steam rose. The creature screeched but still tightened his grip around Aden's neck. Aden walked up the creatures' body as if he was walking up a wall and kicked him in the face as he did a flip and landed on the floor. "Please, please, surely you can understand Queen, that as you want to be bow to…my God works the same way, only he is a jealous God, and it's in his commandments that I bow to only he, and worship no other God, but he. Do you have such rules Queen?"

"I do. Why is your God a jealous God, when there are so many God's among you Beings?" Queen Patano asked.

"There is only one God that I know and worship. I can't speak for others." I said.

"You are a brave and lucky one." Queen Patano chuckled. "I too, understand your God and his ways. Maybe you should maintain inside the realm of your God. But brave you are. Foolish, perhaps I should bow to you, for standing strong for your God." she said.

"No, that is not unnecessary."

"Liliandras will show you to your quarters, Being. Awaiting you are clean garments." I heard a sigh of relief from Aden as I walked passed him. Her home is beautiful on the inside. As I walked down the hallway I saw different pictures, of creatures who seemed to be Queen Patano family. With every step that Liliandras took the floor shook. She looked like Basauras. It reminded me how unusual and out of the normal everything was. I was wondering how we transitioned from a church to a castle. She led me to a room with huge pillars in front of the door. She opened the door and stood humped over, cracked skin and bare foot. She had one braided black patch of hair flowing down her back with an orange ribbon.

"This is your quarter." She said politely. I hesitated to walk near her, this creature was huge. Her arm was bigger than my whole body. Her skin was chapped like winter burned lips. I walked passed her and ran in the room.

"Thank you Liliandras." I know she heard my voice shaking as I closed the door. I stood next to it exhaling as I listened to her footsteps stomping away. I looked around, "She's wealthy all right." I glanced at the gold around the room. I touched the walls which were made up of porcelain. The colors flowed together like a sun over an ocean. I notice a vanity, which held a brush, comb, and ribbon. I stared in the mirror I was dressed in sweats and my hair was tangled in a ponytail. I could just imagine how Aden must have thought of my appearance. Though, I must admit I never seen him look at me, as if he were interested. He seemed aggravated all the time. As a matter of fact, him smirking today was the first time, he seemed amused. Even relaxed. I wonder if he's badly burned or bruised. Is he a creature as what I have been seeing lately? Besides the attraction I have for his lips, and voice, his bent out of shape personality draws me to him. I can't help the magnetic currents between us. He pushes me deeper into a corner and he seems determined to keep me there. I pulled my hair out of a ponytail and I looked around more. There was a tall closet like area and I opened it. There were dresses. They were gorgeous and expensive too. I couldn't believe how beautiful they were. I wanted to try them all at once, but I was a mess. I needed a shower. A knock came to the door and these creatures came in carrying a tub. They dropped it and made a loud thump. One waved its hand, and it filled itself with water. I did not know what to expect next.

****

"Was the fight necessary?" I asked watching Queen Patano and Basauras laugh.

"Aden, I just wanted to see if you maintain your skills in the realm of that Being." Queen Patano laughed.

"Well, I'm glad I passed the test." I said

"Aden, it will take you seven days maybe even ten to journey to your country, my king." Queen Patano said.

"Please, don't call me a king, in front of the Being, Gina." I said.

"But, it would be insolence to call you different."

"It's a personal order, which would be appreciated if you obey." I glanced at her with a look of plea.

"Is that the reason you hide your presence from the Being?"

"What are the safest routes you have planned Lilar?" I said avoiding her question.

"Well sir, you must go through Tanas gate, to Berut Mountains, through Congo plains. This will take you through Sawdawa doors." Lilar said. "There are tents and rests set up for you."

"That's the quickest way." I said

"Yes my king." Lilar responded.

"Don't call me that."

"I apologize, my ruler." Lilar said holding his head down.

"Those are the most shielded parts of Sawdawa. Many different village guards live in the forest and we must pass through quickly. My guards, are they all set to receive us our next stops?" I asked.

"Yes Sire, two of our Elder rulers, Dar and Kilen are waiting your arrival to follow you through Berut Mountains, and through Congo plains."

"Sire, you can't hide from her forever. She will know you soon enough. Her God seems to be powerful, and will show her the way." Queen Patano interrupted, "This is a long way to journey, hidden. And might I add uncomfortable.

"I'm not hiding." I removed the cloak I had around me for days. It felt good to get a flow of air around my body. With this journey we were about to take, I might as well present myself to the Being now.

"Do you think she will not like you for you?"

"I have no interest in her liking me for me. You know where my loyalty lies. Let's end this debate."

"But you can't possible still want to."

"Drop it!" I yelled ending all further talk about the subject with the queen.

"My King, may you remember that your authority is limited, but with all reverence, your father appointed me to give you guidance and protection." Queen Patano said.

"I understand my father's intentions for me and I don't need this." I snapped thinking of the grave responsibility I have ahead of me.

"You will see when the time comes my King, that above all things, I have wisdom. More than you allow yourself to have now." The door opened and Gina walked in. She became accustomed to the present surroundings as well as the garments. Her hair flowed down the sides of her face. She was dressed in a silk gown that fit her body. I never realized her essence before. Her smell captivated me even more than I let it before. It was something about her that even I could not quite understand. I avoided her stare and continued talking strategy. My plans were to keep focused on what my goal was. I had to destroy the She-ad that killed my father, plus get Gina back home to save her friend. Both were a major priority, but I knew deep in my heart revenge was all I was after. I stood paces away as Gina stared out of a window nearby. I heard her thoughts clearly, as if she were talking out loud. All she thought about was Maggie, and why things were happening to her. She didn't complain she was searching to her God for answers and said a prayer over all close to her. She even glanced at me and thanked her God for me, and hoped that we could become friends. She turned away and continued to stare out of the window and her thoughts carried on...

"I wonder why he waited all this time to show himself. Could he not trust me? He acts so nonchalant like nothing matters. Looking at him now, just confuses me. I don't see the reason he was hiding himself. He's gorgeous. Tall, shoulder length black hair, his eyes are funny color. They appear red. He has small cuts across his face, like battle scars. His stature is medium size, and he's muscular. I wonder does he date. How old is he? It would be too intrusive to ask him anything of that nature..."

"Your thoughts are very loud." I told Gina.

"Oh sorry... wait, are you listening to my thoughts?" She asked.

"No not deliberately."

"You are such an ass. How long have you been doing that?"

"You find that annoying? Standing here listening to you is bothersome." I said.

"No wonder you're not close with anyone, you're so nonchalantly evasive..."

"Knowing you, you will find a way to use my ability." I said as she stormed off.

"My king, you shouldn't taunt her." Queen Patano said.

"It wasn't purposely done." I said as Queen Patano gave me a look that will bring even the guiltiest heart to a halt and make it confess. "With flawed efforts, I don't want her to get attached."

"Why?"

"Because I don't want her to it's better to keep her distant."

"Distance will make her more curious than what she already is, Aden?"

"Well, I didn't ask for her to be curious. I didn't ask for her to come around. Now I'm stuck with her through my mission to get rid of that bastard that killed my father." I yelled, and Gina walked into the room as if she was eavesdropping.

"So, you're not helping me. You're just trying to kill someone who killed your father?" Gina said. I said nothing. "What? You didn't want me to hear the truth. My friend is dying and I may never see her again because you will feel guilty if I die on your watch." She cried.

"Gina, you don't." I tried to clean up the mess I made, but she interrupted.

"I want you to take me back home." She stormed out of the room.

"My king, you must ease her thoughts to prepare her for her journey, or this shall distract you on your way." Queen Patano said.
****

Hours after leaving Aden's sight, I couldn't sleep. I cried so much that nothing seemed to fix the pain. There was a knock at my door. I didn't even bother to ask who it was; I knew that they would just come in. I sat in a corner on the floor, with a pillow on my lap. Something small brown, white, and green ran over to me. It had startled me for a moment. It had rubbed its nose on me. It was very friendly.

"He is called Putterball. He is our version, of what you Beings call dogs." Queen Patano said. "Why do you cry being. Have your tears not run dry."

"You would think they would have by now, wouldn't you," I smiled a little wiping my eyes dry.

"Sire Aden doesn't mean to hurt you."

"Aden is a jerk."

"There is a cure for your friend. Even though his reasons were unjust for bringing you here, the cure lies in a forest nearby." Queen Patano said.

"Queen, why is Aden so secretive? Why won't he talk about anything?" I asked.

"Being, Gina! It is not my place to speak for him. But he has experience loss in his life as you. He knows little about befriending anyone." She said.

"Why out of all the planets in the universe, did Nexima come to Earth?" I asked.

"We can go anywhere we choose." Queen Patano said.

"But why Earth?" I asked.

"Earth has more; it is a straight beam of passage for us. And it's a little more advance than any other planet." She said.

"You will find out more about how we transport on your travel."

"How in the world did Sawdawa come to Earth?" I asked

"Our planet is called Nexima, Sawdawa is like our country, and like you Beings have the US of A." Queen Patano said.

"What happened to Aden's father?" I asked, I was full of questions.

"The leader of the she-ads, Ponchopalapare. He invaded Aden's country Sawdawa after losing a war to a nearby country. Aden's father and his army had defeated the She-ads twice. One night, there was an ambush on his village and his father was murdered in front of him when he was fifteen eras. Since then he had been cursed, never to be able to touch anything like Skins, or in Being form without burning them, there was said to be a cure, but only his father knew what it was. His father knew what caused the curse, no one else did."

"How old is he?" I asked.

"Three-hundred eras."

"Three-hundred years old!" I said.

"He had vowed from that moment to destroy, Ponchopalapare."

"What about his mother?"

"His mother disappeared without a trace eras before his father died."

"He has lived this long, with no one?" I asked as Putterball jumped in my lap.

"No one, but me and a few others whom all vow to fight against the She-ads, until every last one is extinct." Queen Patano said.

"I should have known something has made Aden the way he is."

"I see you have had trouble also in your eras." Queen Patano said

"Yes, how do you know of my past?"

"I'm like you beings crystal ball talkers." She struggled to find the right words.

"Why hasn't Aden married and started his own family? And why was he in exile on earth?"

"Being that is another discussion for another time and day. You rest. You have a long journey ahead of you. Come Putterball." She said as the creature jumped off my lap and followed behind her.

"Join us in the common room for a feast at daybreak, Being. You will be at ease." I watched Queen Patano leave with Putterball behind her. I climbed into bed, tucking myself under thick pieces of silk. It seems to be all that Queen Patano used in her home. There were so many lines on the ceiling, I counted them before falling asleep. I dreamt of running with my arms stretched out. I reached for something. It wasn't clear at all. There was smoke and fire in the background. My hands and arms were cut up. Then it came, a huge creature, with a horn in the middle of his head. The image had awakened me out of my sleep. "This trip will be long and I don't know what to expect from it." I said.

It was daylight outside, and it was new clothing hanging next to the vanity. I heard no one come in. This gown was red and gold. The sleeves to the dress were long, and the length stop short at the knees. There was hot steaming water in a bowl which could be a sink. Next to it was a round material that looked like a large sponge, and round shape fruit. When I touched it, it opened with sugs, it was fruit with a perfume fragrance. I couldn't make out the scent, but it was a wonderful relaxing smell. It smelled like warm butterscotch, and crème. After getting dressed, I hesitated to step out of the privacy and comfort of the room, but I decided not to keep myself locked up. After debating about if I would talk to Aden, I went to join everyone in the common room. I walked down the long hallway only to be greeted by Aden.

"You appear well rested." He said as we walked.

"Well enough." I tried not to be angry.

"I can hear that you're still angry in your tone."

"Well, don't talk to me, and I won't have to respond, and you won't hear the anger in my voice."

"I regret both of our miss direction to the course of our lives. I'll give you distance, enjoy the daybreak." He said.

Later that day I sat in the common room, next to Basauras and Putterball, as Aden, and Lilar discuss the routes to Sawdawa. Basauras gave me a shot that was to help me from getting sick as we traveled. I saw Lilar and had paid little attention to him. He was short with gray hair, and he had something over his eyes it appeared to be skin framed around his eyes like glasses. He was a creature with big huge dried bumps on his yellow face. Aden only talked to Lilar to avoid looking at me. It didn't matter I was happy. I didn't want him talking, looking or even breathing in my direction. I was still angry with him for his self-interest, but he apologized. I was angry with him.

"It is sunset Aden you must be on your way." Queen Patano walked in.

"I'm getting everything ready now Patano." Aden said bowing to her.

"My sweet Gina, Be brave for we should meet soon enough." She said grabbing my hand.

"Thank you for your hospitality." I said.

"Remember distance will make you more curious Aden." Queen Patano said.

"Bye." Aden wrapped his cloak around him and got into the car. Before I close the door, Putterball came strutting and I patted him on what seem to be his head.

"Get, Putterball." Aden said aggressively.

I protectively clicked the seat belt together. A bright light shined and we flew through the wall and on our journey we went. The car was quiet. There was no sound for about two hours. He avoided my stare, and I avoided his. Someone had to break the silence.

"So where are we headed?" I asked.

"So she speaks?" he smirked.

"Does that bother you?"

"No. It's better than the silence."

"Wow, so the silent treatment bothered you?" I laughed.

"What's amusing about that?" He looked curiously.

"It always works with guys."

"I'm not like the male species in your world."

"All species have similarities." I said. "So the silent treatment should bother you."

"Do you want to know where we're going or not?" Aden said avoiding my comment.

"Yeah." I smiled.

"Go ahead."

"It will take us about six days to get to Sawdawa, if nothing interferes with the travel. We will travel through a place call Tanas gate, to Berut Mountains, through the Congo plains, which will take us to the Sawdawa doors." He said.

"So how long will it take us to bring the medicine back?" I asked.

"About three days. It's quicker leaving Nexima realm than it is coming. There are different energy tones."

"What are energy tones?" I asked.

"Energy tones are portals that are only open through beams from our sun during certain times. These beams have different patterns and heat sources. A straight beam goes to a different planet with a cool temperature source. A cross beam goes to the planet farthest from our universe and it has a heat source that no one can survive going through, but specific breeds and vertical beam goes to Earth with a heat source weak enough for everyone to travel. These beams also break up into others travel points." Aden spoke.

"Will Maggie be able to fight the illness for this long?"

"It depends on her will to live."

"The illness is going to be painful for her… Isn't it?"

"Yes. It will be. I believe she can hold on. If she's your friend and is as strong as you are, she will be ok." He said.

"You gave me a compliment. That's new." He said nothing and smiled a little. It was silence for a minute and his smiled lasted a while. I looked out of the window. I could do nothing but smile. This is a different person from whom I met a few days prior. I want to get to Aden's home get the medicine and get back to my life. I wish I could change things, but if I did this whole moment with Aden, would have never happened. I would never have felt this safe and happy like I do right now with him.

Chapter 4: Midnight Run in the Forest

We traveled for hours, but it felt like days. We had passed through different climate changes, from cold to freezing rain. When we left the state approaching another, the sign welcomed us to Indiana, but I had to do a double take because another sign said the Great Tanas Forest. I had never seen that sign before traveling through Indiana. I must admit after receiving that shot Basauras gave me, I could see things clearly. Were my eyes opening up to things that had already been, and I just never noticed? I turned to Aden, he wasn't driving the car. The Nitzer was steering itself. When we left Queen Patano, the light shined so brightly I had no choice but to shield my eyes in defense of it, but when I opened my eyes we were traveling on the road. There was a portal exchange, but I didn't remember seeing it. Things were definitely becoming weird. This brings me to realization of how out of my grasp everything was. I'm noticing that this Nitzer is transportation through the gates of his world. Every place we stopped was a base to prepare us for the travel to his world. It was somewhat of resting areas for humans who had to make stops when they traveled out of town. I looked at Aden; he had laid back in his seat. I never knew he slept. His face was covered with the hood of his cloak. He loved the dark for some reason. I took my eyes off him, "What is that?" I said noticing ahead of the road; it was something huge and metal like standing straight in the lanes. "Aden. Aden, wake up" I yelled to wake him as the car automatically shift to the side.

"What is it?" he said as the car shut off.

"What is going on? What is that?"

"That is a tree." He said mockingly.

"What is a metal tree doing in the middle of the road? And how does the car steer itself? And why did the car shut off?"

"So many questions... and I haven't a clue." Aden said turning and pushing buttons.

"It's quiet, and dark. Are the doors locked?" I said looking around.

"For my fellow unknown species a locked car will not help." Aden smirked, he was quiet, he flicked the car brights on and tried starting the car back up. The car lights shut off his eyes shifted slowly behind me. "This is not good." Aden said.

"What's not good Aden?" I asked.

"Don't move and don't get out of the car. Stare straight at me. Do not turn around."

I turned around anyway from pure panic and there stood a giant blob of something grayish blue. Its eyes were split into the skin with little insect legs embedded around them. Its mouth stretched wide open and screeched. The sound was deafening as hit the top of the car. It tossed us towards the tree, a flash of lightning spark and exploded like thunder. We were in a forest. The trees were bright green, they appeared out of nowhere. We flew into another creature, it opened its eyes. It pounded on the hood. One was pulling off the trunk and the other the hood. I screamed as the car was being yanked back and forth.

"Stop screaming. Just calm down." Aden said.

"How am I supposed to calm down when I'm about to die?"

"The more you scream, the angrier they get. Jump out of the car and run and I will be right behind you." Aden said as the car dropped to the ground.

"Are you crazy?" I yelled.

"Stay in this car a few seconds more and you will die. Do as I said."

"Oh! I hate my life." I reached for the door handle and tried to open it, but it was stuck. "It's stuck." I turned and realized I was talking to no one. "Aden I'm stuck. Aden. Oh Lord, help me."

"Hey! Over here." Aden yelled to the creatures. "That's right, come get your meal." Both the creatures focused on Aden as their target and tossed the car with me in it effortlessly. I hit my head. I tried clearing my head from the impact. It took a minute. I climbed over to Aden's side of the car and tried to get out, but that door was stuck too. The car caught fire. I kicked at the door, pushed it, and pulled the handle, but it wouldn't bulge. There was blood running down my face. The smoke from the fire got heavy. I called to Aden, but he was fighting the creatures. The car door swung open. I jumped out of the car. I ran behind a rock. I sat up and watched as he went toe to toe with these creatures. One had him down on the ground. His body lit, like a match for a split second and one creature caught fire. The other, Aden just picked up and threw down. He leaped up and grabbed the biggest branch from one of the forest trees. I blinked for a moment and Aden was gone. I coughed because the car was still smoking and on fire about ten feet from me.

"Are you done dying?" Aden said holding his shoulder.

"Yeah." I said coughing.

"Let's get out of here." He said walking towards the car.

"That thing is going to blow."

"Give it a few minutes it will." He said grabbing a bag out of the front seat. He walked away from the car smooth as ever. I ran behind him wondering what would happen next. A few minutes walking and the car surely blew. The explosion was loud and you could feel the heat, the ground shook, and you could still smell the smoke. Suddenly I took it upon myself to rest and sat on top of a rock holding my head.

"Is everything always like this with you?" I asked holding my head. "What were those things?"

"Those were Kinzel Guardians. They protect the entrance to my world. You're bleeding." Aden said.

"Being tossed around in a car will do that to you." I responded. "What about you?"

"I'm fine! Listen. When I tell you don't scream, or tell you to jump. I mean don't scream, and I mean jump." He snapped.

"You are used to this stuff, I'm not. So excuse the hell out of me if I'm disturbed about things I've never seen before! And the freaking door was stuck, give me some credit." I said watching Aden pace back and forth.

"We need to keep moving to get to the next rest stop. You Beings are very difficult. It's your resolve under pressure that gets you out of situations."

"Don't say Beings like that. I'm a person with a name. And you're practically human too aside from a bunch of fire coming out of your ass. And I mean that metaphorically and literally." I snapped. He said nothing he just walked, and I followed behind him. Every time I checked my watch it said the same time. I had no knowledge, of time. I was angry, tired and cold. Now I really wish my life could go back to the way it was.

****

A night in the Tanas Forest would be difficult, especially walking on foot. I could get there quicker gliding, but I had to settle by foot, because I can't touch Gina to carry her the rest of the way. I turned to see her dragging behind me, she was tired but there was no time to rest. I had noticed that she was becoming more aware that she wasn't in her world anymore, and the next steps we take, things that she didn't understand would become transparent to her. I knew that a swarm of creatures were on the rise looking through this forest to stop me from getting to Tanas Gate. I noticed that the gates were more guarded than they ever were. I suspect that this is to keep the She-ads at bay to stop them from traveling to Earth. I have a lot of enemies, and most of them wanted my throne. A throne I wish I never had. I have no clue how to lead anyone, or how to be a King. I had a few miles to go before I got to Dar. I would really need him for the journey through the end of this forest.

"I need to rest Aden." Gina said.

"Gina, we need to get to the next stop, it's not that far."

"You said that however many minutes ago I asked you." She said.

"You asked two hours ago, but we are almost there."

"I can't walk anymore." She sat on the ground.

"Gina! Get up. This is the time I need you to push yourself. Don't do this right now. It's not safe just to sit in the open like this." I said watching our surroundings.

"You have super powers; protect me if something goes wrong. Give me two minutes?"

"I'm not flash; I can't go for a midnight run in this forest, without being cautious." He said. There was a cracking sound in the bushes. It was scurrying footsteps. Whatever it was began circling us. The smell was familiar. I could make out they were speed demons. They were the same size if not a little taller than I. They weighed approximately three-hundred pounds. They were too swift to be seen with one glance. Speed demons were creatures that are ancestors of Phantoms. They were born guards of all forests surrounding Nexima walls. Their skin has spikes embedded in them. They are muscular and they can stretch their arms for many distances. They glide and are trained in the art of Klitzo. Klitzo is staph weaponry.

"What is that noise?" Gina said standing up, she searched the area for the noise as she moved closer to me.

"Don't move." I told her. It was two of them. I shifted from the ground, raising myself, showing my ability to what humans would call flying to see over the bushes. They were fast. I could see them running in circles. I landed on my feet. "Stay here, don't move Gina." I glided through the trees. I tried to follow the course of the demons. I stopped as my hearing clicked into the paused footsteps, and ran back to Gina. One appeared in front of her before I could stand protectively next to her. She screamed and tried to run. He stretched to grab her and then pulled her towards him. He lifted her up wrapping both hands around her throat, choking her. She struggled to get loose. "I would let her go if I were in your position." I yelled to the speed demon choking her, as I watched her kick for air.

"So we meet again Prince Bartarino." The creature said.

"Long time no see Colar. Put her down."

"Why are you in these woods Bartarino?"

"I'm just passing through. There's no harm in that Colar." I said as the other demon stood behind me.

"Well, The King re-appears, after thirty eras." The second demon spoke with a whisper that sounded like a growl.

"Hello to you too Heigra." I shifted to both demons so they both were in my eyesight. Gina had stopped struggling, she was losing consciousness. "How are you in these quarters? I ask for the last time let her go."

"Why would you bring a Being, in these quarters?" Colar asked.

"I said I'm passing through. Now I asked for the last time let her go." Gina hands had already fallen from Colars hands around her neck. Colar dropped her.

"I will take great joy in killing the King Colar." Heigra growled making his stave appear. My hands had lit forming a burst of fire, as they charged me. Heigra ran and swung his stave. I caught it making it as hot as possible with the flames from my hands. Colar grabbed me from the back and I struggled. My body lit like a force field throwing Colar back. I snatched the staph from Heigra, using him as a step stool to fly over Colar and I landed behind him. I swung the heated stick knocking Heigra down and stabbed Colar through the chest. Colar screeched, but in anger not pain. Heigra laughed and pulled the stick from Colar's body. Colar jumped and deeply gashed my arm with his sharpen claws. Heigra beat my leg until I fell, shoving the stave into it. I yelled with pain. I was weakening. This fight was longer than I expected. I fell backwards. Colar and Heigra stood over me. Colar grabbed me by the neck inserting his nails deep into my skin. An emerald dagger shot through the both of them. They screamed and collapsed. Seconds later two creatures stood over them ending the fight.

"My king, are you okay?"

"Dar, the Being." I pointed to Gina whom was sprawl out on the ground.

"Yes my king, Kilen came from Congo Plains because he felt you were in extreme danger. Kilen will help you. I will take care of the Being." Dar said.

Dar and Kilen were my father's most trusted guards and now are mine, and they are set up in Tanas Forest, for whenever I should return home. Dar was a Skin with four arms, and two legs. He was tall and muscular, a very brave warrior. He was a friend of my mother. Kilen was a full-blooded Phantom three-thousand eras. He's the wisest elder, and he never talks. Dar carried Gina to the rest that awaited us. Gina never moved, and never noticed that we moved swiftly to the rest. This rest differed greatly from the other. It was a small cabin like on the outside, but there were tall ceilings and enough rooms on the inside to house twenty Nexima families. Dar and Kilen kept this place well protected because it was their home away from home. I used Kilen to lean on getting the rest of the way. Gina wasn't awake yet, she hadn't move the whole walk to the rest. When we entered, and she was laid down, she didn't move and couldn't notice her surroundings.

"Make sure she's breathing?" I said to Dar as I sat holding my side.

"The Being still breathes your highest." Dar said. I sat on the silk bed she laid on I was weakening every second I stood, blood running down my body. My body started reconstructing itself. The pain was intense. There was no cure for me; I had to take the time to heal on my own.

"Put me in another room Kilen. Now!" I said. Kilen glanced at me with his ability to transport, the next second I was in a concrete room stretched out. The wounds stretched and pulled itself back together. The blood turned into foam. Mentally the healing takes a toll, my vision blurred, and my hearing distant. Everything became dark.

Early the next daybreak, I walked into the room Gina was resting in she had not awaken yet. I was getting accustom to seeing her. Strangely, knowing she would be there when I turned the corner made me excited to see another day. I don't like to admit that to myself because that puts her in more danger, and knowingly I would allow it. It was taking her so long to wake up it bothered me. Seeing the life being sucked out of her and not being able to help her tortured me as I slept. I kept seeing her face unconscious. I sat in a chair next to her. I watched her. I heard her breathing, and her heart beating. But she hadn't wakened.

As I watched her, I saw her beauty with every blink of my eye. Her hair was curly from the moisture in the forest air, and for a brief moment I wanted to run my fingers through it. She had a cut on the side of her face that wasn't healing, and it was the only wound I wanted to heal. I felt her pain every second as she grieved for her friend, like I grieved for my father. Still, she didn't move. She breathed in and out. I felt the rhythm of heartbeat. So I stared. This feeling I was having I didn't know, but whatever it was, at this time, and moment, I liked it.

****

I opened my eyes, finding myself in another exotic room. I looked around at all the colors and smelling the fresh flowers and when I glanced to the side I seen Aden sitting, staring at me. He had such a concern look on his face. He smirked a little with a relief, "Are you all right?" He asked.

"I'm awake, so I guess you can say so." I said sitting up. I grabbed my head; it throbbed with so much pain, like tons of rocks had been tossed at it. "Where are we?" I asked looking around.

"The next rest stop." He starred.

"What's wrong?" I asked releasing my hand from my head, looking at his worried face.

"Why would you ask that?" He stood up and turned away.

"What's wrong?"

"Nothing."

"You look like you want to say something."

"I guess my world is rubbing off on you because you now have the ability of mind reading."

"What happen last night?"

"Just two old friends showed up."

"You called them friends, they tried to kill me."

"The interaction of those speed demons trying to kill me would be normal warrior conversation. You're a Being. You're not supposed to be in this world." He said walking next to the window.

"What do you mean this world? I was born on Earth. We are still on Earth aren't we?"

"You're not on Earth's world anymore. When we pass through these rest, which you call rest stops you may not notice, but you're passing through transition into my world. Your world becomes an illusion, and my world becomes real. That shot that Basauras gave you was not to stop you from getting sick, but to allow your body to go through all these different atmospheric changes."

"Where am I?" I asked.

"Nexima!" he said.

"What's that?"

"That's the name of my world, my planet, my country etc..."

"Will there be more things trying to kill me because I'm an outsider?"

"Probably." I noticed he smirked as he looked outside of a huge window. It seemed we were on like the fortieth floor because it was a long way to fall.

"Are we at Tanas Gate?"

"We are in Tanas Gate. We have a ways to go to Berut Mountains." There was knocking at the door.

"Come in."

"Sir, you have awaited guests." Dar said.

"Guests?" I asked looking at Aden.

"I will see you soon Gina. Thank you Dar." Aden walked to the door.

"If we are going to get you to Berut Mountains in good timing, we must leave soon. The journey is long."

"Thank you Dar." Aden whispered.

"Gina." Dar said bowing his head.

"Aden, why does everyone call you sire?" I asked.

"It's for respect of my father." He said and the door closed after his words. Things seemed a little weird, I didn't know what to think and what to believe anymore. Aden walked around with this new found glory where everyone worshipped him, but there are more things that hate him. I was caught in the middle. I wasn't supposed to be in this world and it was now evident. I slipped out of the room to see where I was I came across this room where there were calm voices and they were greeting Aden, and Dar. I just stood and listened.

"Hello." Aden spoke to them as they bowed.

"You have returned. It is I Rolion, ruler of Sagela." Rolion said.

"And I Magolonia. Watcher of the gates." Magolonia said.

"Welcome. What brings you?" Dar asked.

"We are here to guide you to the rests of the gates per requests of Queen Patano." Rolion said.

"We will be ready to leave soon." Aden said. I saw Aden's nose flare, I knew he could tell my scent, and he walked his guests to another room and they closed the door. I wondered what would be discussed, but eventually I would find out. A few hours later we all journey on our path to get to Berut Mountains. We took a well-lit path through the forest. Aden said we had to carry on by foot because the Nitzer would not carry Dar. I noticed every time we moved we stepped in a pile of insects. When you stepped down the bugs would jump and land on another and they would light the path. We had four new creatures with us. Rolion he was similar looking to Dar but he was much taller and instead of having four arms he had two and four legs. He bore a symbol above his right gray eye. His attire was of wealth similar to Aden. His weapon was a staph with a blade at the end and he had holster with viles, knives, and pockets. He had no shoes, his feet were wide, and he had three toes and they were covered with hair. Dar had no hair, but Rolion did. The sides of his head were shaved, but he had long gray hair down the center of his head. As Aden followed behind him occasionally I had seen things, like a ghost. I couldn't figure out what it was.

"That's Kilen Gina." Aden said without looking back

"Stop reading my thoughts Aden." I whispered.

"Don't think so loud Gina." He laughed as well as Dar. Aden was loosening up, and for a minute I thought we were becoming friends. Dar walked on the side of me and Magolonia in the back of me. He had three eyes. One was in the center of his face above his mouth, his nose was encrusted above the eye. He was huge, and he scared me. His hair was like the skin from his head was melting, the skin just drooped down. He wore no shirt, and his pants covered his feet as if they were shoes. His chest had war marks and symbols. His ears were pierced with little blades inside them. I looked back at him and he stared with disgust on his face and I turned around and sped up to walk closely to Aden, to stay as far away from him as possible. Aden looked back at me and he gave the exact look he was giving me as when I had awakened. That same glance when I opened my eyes, was as if he was feeling a lot of compassion. I liked this side of him. I still know very little about him. I only know he doesn't like people, and he lost all of his family. I know there are things he holds back about himself, and I know its things he wants to say, but he bites his tongue. I wonder when he will open up. He puts his life on the line time and time again for me. I think of him as my personal super hero. I wish that Maggie had a chance to get to the know Aden, and right now, I don't know if she ever will.

Chapter 5: Someone to Trust

"Dear one, are you cold?" Dar asked me as I shivered.

"Is it that obvious?" I responded as Dar dug in a bag he carried and pulled out a silk blanket and wrapped it around me. "Thank you."

"You are but most welcomed. I must ask for forgiveness to ask this, but you seem sadden, no?"

"Yes. Well, I feel alone. No friends here and I'm out of place. My best friend is sick and dying all because of me. I feel awful."

"Gina, some things are not in our abilities to control. This was meant to happen." Dar looked at me.

"What do you mean, like fate? You honestly believe that?" I shook my head with doubt.

"I do, history and Time repeats itself. Someday, someone was meant to discover our lands and this world and fate chose you."

"Fate?" I asked.

"Dar, gather food for Gina." Aden appeared with a warning in his tone. Dar rose and bowed hustling away as Aden sat next to me. He pointed to the flame that was dying around the sticks and relit them with a wave of his palm. "You are troubled?" He asked.

"A little. Thanks for lighting that." I said as Aden smile a bit. We sat in silence. I had no clue what to say to him. I was always worried about what his response would be.

"Gina do you always carrying on a conversation with your thoughts, or do you speak at some point?" Aden stared at me.

"I do. And who are these people?" I looked around at small fires burning and dozens of tiny clusters of creatures in different groups sitting around each one.

"These are Rolions people. They protect this domain of the forests. Each creature of our world have a piece of the borders to protect."

"So the entry to Earth and Nexima is that big?" I asked looking around.

"Yes, enormous, I believe is the proper word to use, in this case." I looked to my right and Magolonia was watching me. I swear he was making me nervous. Aden looked to him and Magolonia looked away. "Do not fear him. He has never seen a Being before. He watches you in disbelief and is studying you." Aden smiled. "He actually thinks you are fascinating and Neckglacimas."

"What does Neckglacimas mean?" I looked at Aden for an answer.

"A beautiful creature." I looked at Aden as his smile faded as he watched him, and he turned to give a reassuring smile that everything was ok, but something happened. I could sense it. Dar approached with some food. "Stay amongst her, do not let her out of your sight." Dar exchanged looks with Aden as he turned from him and walked away. Words just spoken between them. But what were they?

"What was that about?" I asked.

"Oh, worry not. Here, eat." Dar handed me a bowl of things I've never seen since I've been in this world. I refrain from eating much here.

"What is this?"

"Taste for they are sweet." I ate and each portion resembles the sweetness of strawberries and sour like green grapes from home, so they were fruits. After eating, I needed some sleep. "This shelter has been set up for you. It will be great winds tonight and you will not sleep well out in the open. I noticed this small tent. It was cold, but I did not want to go in alone. "Do not be afraid, I will not leave your side. Rest young one." Dar said.

I walked in and it was huge on the inside. A bed sat in the corner in front of a fireplace. There were rugs on the floor, a table and chairs. Clothes were hung up for when I wake in the morning. I looked out of the tent and Dar sat guarding the doorway. I crawled into the bed and wrapped myself with all the silk blankets and I drifted. I dreamt that Magolonia stood above me watching me. He was observing me from head to feet and when I opened my eyes he attacked me. I jumped from sleeping and I was covered in sweat and Dar walked in.

"Are you ok?"

"I'm fine, a bad dream." I rubbed sweat from my face.

"It's late. Rest, you are well guarded. Would you like me to stay at your side until you fall asleep?"

"It will help me rest. Please." I felt like a kid. This was something my dad use to do, he use to sit at my side until I fell asleep. Dar pulled a chair to my bedside and sat. Dar sang. It was a beautiful song. The melody reminded me of something. He sang it in his language. "Si no, mak me, so voy ya me. Qew, que me voy soy ya me." Dar sang, and I drifted again as his words became soft and sweet to my ears. It was as if they helped me sleep. I dreamt of my parents, how they both at one point in my life tucked me in and my mom sang to me before things got bad. She sang, "Please sleep, sleep, your dreams will bring you peace. Tomorrow will bring you peace." The melody Dar sang reminded me much of her song. I opened my eyes to a whisper and Aden sat next to me.

"Gina!" He whispered.

"Yes! What's wrong?"

"I do not mean to wake you, but we must be on our way. Please prepare yourself for the day." He looked as if he got no rest at all. His eyes had dark circles around them. He walked out of the tent and I gather my thoughts and got ready. I sneezed repeatedly and I had a pounding headache. This looked like the beginning to a horrible cold.

****

We waited for Gina and she finally stumbled out of her quarters, falling on the ground. Dar was at her side aiding her. She sat for a minute as I watched him talk to her. He was so fond of her and treated her as if she was a child of his. He wrapped a blanket around her to shield her from the frigid air. He walked over.

"Sire, the Being she is ill." Dar said as we looked at her holding her head.

"What is wrong with it?" Rolion asked.

"She will be fine. It is what a Being calls a cold." I spoke.

"It's cold." Rolion asked.

"No as we get sick from diseases. She has what is called a cold. Let's go." I walked over to Gina. She looked awful. She was sweating profusely. "Are you able to walk?"

"Do I have a choice?" She asked sarcastically. Her voice wasn't even the same.

"Dar, is there a way to communicate with Lilar?" I asked.

"No sire." Dar said as he helped Gina up. "She burns, her skin burns."

"It's a fever." Gina said. Everyone looked at her.

"Fever?" Rolion said.

"What?" A guard said.

"What is that?" Magolonia asked.

"Nothing. We have to leave now." My patients grew short because the guards were thinking of killing her from fear of diseases. Creatures here feared diseases more than anything. They watched her as she coughed and how red her face had become. They talked under their breaths. We moved through the forests quickly. Gina was a hindrance. Dar had to pick her up and carry her. She slept in his arms. She coughed and made a sound she called a sneeze. I didn't realize Beings had so many side effects to something so common. A couple hours went by, a GonaGone, whom Gina wondered in her thoughts if he was a doctor. He came from the lands of Rolion. His name was Thunderos. He was a Diminutive, short and had long yellow hair, and bruises on his face from old age. With him, he had many vials of liquid. He shooked his head at Gina grabbing a little vial and inserted liquids from each vial into it. His wide hand shook the vial. He looked at Gina sweating, he took a syringe and filled it with the liquid and inserted it into Gina's chest.

"She needs to rest before going into the cold again."Thunderos said.

"How long will this Being hold us?" Rolion asked walking in.

"Maybe three moments to hours."He said. "Aden, walk with me." Thunderos said. We walked out of the tent. He stood and looked up at me. "I know not what effects this medicine will have on her. These are cures for our race of creatures, not Beings."

"You mean to tell me, this may not be a good thing. That she could die?" I asked.

"Symptoms are similar to the Kinzuma, the mutating disease. But I cannot guarantee results." He said and he walked away. I looked into the tent and Gina laid asleep. I couldn't believe everything that was happening. Rolion walked over as I watched Dar sit beside Gina.

"We can take you to the step of the sands. We can go no further." Rolion said.

"Why is that?" I looked at him.

"I fear that there may be many of us that hearts are too tortured to cross the sands. For that reason, we cannot cross without harm." He spoke in a soft voice.

I let his words trail to the back of my mind as I listened to Dar and Gina talk. She sounded like she couldn't breathe. She and Dar shared many things, a little about her family. But Dar told jokes to make her feel comforted. She laughed. He listened as she shed tears for her friend. But yet in still, he comforted her. They were becoming close. As she drifted to sleep, Dar sat by her side patiently. He didn't move. He held her hand and watched her. I heard Magolonia thoughts. He wanted badly to get near the Being, to smell her scent to just stare at her beauty. Others wondered why I would risk my life for her. Others spoke about how they hated to serve her, a filthy creature. But Magolonia got deeper thoughts from his heart wished he didn't feel that way about an outlawed creature. He wish she would go away. I watched him closely as he walked by her tent and stared in. He knew I was watching, he knew that any wrong move he made, it would be severe consequences. Yet he stared for a moment and walked away. Yet, there was another who was feeling great agony for Gina's presence.

Chapter 6: The Sand in front of the Gates

The next morning I felt better. It seemed as if I was never sick. We began our journey onward walking in the forest. I was exhausted, and truth be told it felt like we were walking forever. The creatures that visited Aden tagged along for extra protection and guidance. I still kept my distance from Magolonia as he still watched me. Things were so quiet I swear I could hear every animal in the forest breathe.

"How far are the gates from here Dar?" Aden asked.

"We have a short distance Sir." Dar responded.

"Ok, you guys keep saying that every twenty minutes." I snapped climbing a hill.

"How do you know the moment Being?" Rolion asked.

"I count the seconds in my head, like a human would. And… I've been climbing this same hill forever." I said.

"We should keep moving sir; Kilen and the others grow protective of our surroundings." Dar pointed to Kilen who is above us guarding our surroundings, reminding us he was still present.

"Strange this is, if I'm not mistaking one of King Griven kingdoms is before the gates. This is unusual we traveled through Tanas and have seen none of his kingdom men." Aden said looking straight ahead.

"Dar and I will get you through." Kilen said swooping down, gliding as we walked, startling me.

"We have befriended those at the gates."

"Except the sand will falls deep. It daunts upon all with an uneasy heart." Dar said.

"Let's be on our way then." Aden said ignoring the extreme warning that was spoken. I couldn't understand half of what was spoken between them; they all spoke in codes, and metaphors. Their language was hard to grasp, but Aden over looks things. I noticed things seem to personal or just bothersome to him. I now characterize Aden as the, "I laugh in the face of danger type of guys."

"Dar position yourself to the back." Aden said.

Dar walked behind me and Aden on my side. Dar walked behind us and guarded. Kilen circled around, practically invisible the whole time. Rolion and Magolonia walked in front of us and other guards behind us. I became cautions with my thoughts. I repeated a tune in my head over and over. Aden laughed.

"What's so funny?" I asked.

"I don't do it on purpose, you know." Aden smiled. Suddenly I felt it. It was such a warm and lovable quality about him.

"Do what on purpose?" I asked.

"Hear your thoughts."

"So you can't stop it?" I asked.

"Not if I wanted to." He said.

"What else can you do?"

"Besides the impeccable hearing and blowing fire out my ass?"

"Yeah." I blushed.

"I wouldn't be, how do you say, a mystery if I told you."

"Why do you want to be a mystery?"

"There are things about me I don't want eyes to be observant to. Exactly like your thoughts."

"What does that mean?" I was confused

"Private. I would like to remain private."

"Have you ever, once in the three-hundred years you've been living, enjoyed anything or been nice to anyone?" I asked.

"Queen Patano! She's extremely talkative." Aden turned away and shook his head.

"Yes... don't change the subject. She told me many things. A little girl talk."

"No. Enjoying things is not a luxury I have. I've been forced into the life that has seemed to become." Aden said.

"Have you ever..." I stop talking.

"Ever what...? Love someone?" Aden finished my sentence, invasively reading my thoughts.

"Yeah." I responded.

"I... wouldn't want to put someone in danger all the time because of my decisions I make. And you?"

"No one."

"That's hard to understand." He said.

"Why is that hard to believe?"

"Not hard to believe. Hard to understand. You're…"

"I'm what?"

"Nothing!" Aden said briefly blushing, catching himself.

"No, just say what you were going to say."

"You're a beautiful Being. I can't understand why?"

I didn't know how to respond to his comment. I was flushed. It became hot, and I was walking in the cold of the forest. There was silence between us for a few minutes.

"I have a boring life." I said "I need a little more excitement. Who knows maybe one day?" We walked the rest of the way in silence. I smiled for a while, with the feel of my cheeks becoming numb. The woods were still, and all that was heard was the whistling of the wind, the sticks that was stepped on, and the heavy breathing that Dar was doing. I looked to the sky and there were stars, but instead of being bright white they were orange. I wanted to make a wish, but maybe these weren't wishing stars. Aden glanced up above for a second, smiled and pretended not to look my way. He was reading my thoughts again. He gave me a compliment; I could let this one slide. Just this once.

"We will not go any further." Rolion stopped.

"May you be protected sire." Magolonia bowed.

"Thank you all very much." I said.

Suddenly we exited the forest onto an island of sand viewing further ahead a giant gate with armed guards. We walked toward the gate feeling the sand beneath our feet. Kilen had glided to the front as Dar stood behind Gina and me. It was something different about the sand in these parts. I had never seen it so dark and red. The atmosphere seemed dead. The air smelt stale. Something wasn't right. I remember the sand being a beautiful yellow color with no impurities.

"Wait here!" Kilen said gliding further ahead to greet the guards of Tanas Gates.

"I'm stuck." Gina yelled as the sands reacted in a vine pulling her in.

"We're sinking in." I yelled.

"Aden, I'm going into quicksand. Help" Gina yelled.

"It's okay Gina. Just relax, keep your mouth and eyes closed." I said.

"Aden."

"Trust me."

"No, no! Get me out of here."

"Silent Being the Kings advice is good for you." Kilen said gliding over as we sank into the sand. Gina eyes were shut and she fell through the sand. Dar tried grabbing me, but the sand had already pulled me straight through. I landed on solid ground. Gina sat up coughing and spitting up sand. I stood, on guard from whatever came our way.

"My king, you have return, unharmed." I looked towards the raspy voice at a face partially sparkling with sand dust sitting on a throne was Prince Griven.

"I'm sure that bothers you Prince Griven." I said.

"Kilen said King? You're a king?" Gina asked as she stood up.

"You do not speak Being until spoken to." Prince Griven yelled.

"Be calm Griven, this is my guest." I said.

"Ha, are you infatuated with this Being, Aden. When Love awaits you?" Prince Griven said. Griven was made of sand and skin. A sand demon was what my father told me made the likes of Griven. He had a very thin build. Sand Demons are creatures full of tricks. They can transform into anything they like.

They are taught rituals using sand. Their power is their sand, Klitzo and fighting skills. He is the son of King Griven. He sat upon a metal sand stone throne. His home was underground. The walls were mirror like, but metal. It was cool in there. There were many halls that separated the inside of his home. As I looked at him, he was short with a cocky attitude. We have always been enemies since infancy. He couldn't stand I had beaten him in everything. But I think his defeats are formed from, him and his father, wanting to acquire greatness the easy way. "I always wondered how you can govern a whole country without being present, young Aden." Prince Griven asked sliding as a pile of dust towards me.

"The same way you and your father can ruin a nation, Prince Griven?" I watched Griven circle us.

"I'll ask you one question; you must answer truthfully because my sand knows an uneasy heart." Prince Griven said

"I don't have time for any competitions." I said.

"You will do as I say, or you won't pass. Aden Bartarino." He mocked. "A whole kingdom and you didn't earn it. It fell into your lap."

"Are we bitter Griven? I can't help that your father still roams this world… I've heard chubby and despondent."

"I see through you now." Prince Griven laughed and held his stave. "You will answer the question."

"Ask away?" I said.

"Has corruption grabbed your heart?"

"Corruption? What is he talking about?" Gina asked.

"It depends on the corruption you speak, Griven?"

"Don't play coy with me. The games you played in that Beings world, doesn't work here. Now answer the question."

"I say once again, what corruption do you speak of?" I asked.

"A king between two….?"Prince Griven said.

"Yes!" I said cutting him short.

"You may try to disguise it now Aden dear boy, but it will appear in the open." Prince Griven said.

"Let me through the gates."

"Now that would be to easy would it not?" Prince Griven said.

"The easier the better. I do not have aggression towards your village. It would be wise to let me through the gates or harm will surely invade your sands." I said.

"Aden, do you think your threats bother me… a denial prince! I obey one king. My father, whom you should pass once you exit Tanas Gates. For now he rules half of your Berut Mountains." Prince Griven said.

"Aden is there anyone here who is your friend?" Gina whispered.

"Disobedient speaking Being, make sure you say a big hello to Nirew." Prince Griven smirked.

"Open the gates" I yelled.

"As my would be King wishes." Prince Griven laughed sarcastically raising his stave, and the sand separated above us like huge doors. "I enjoy these times with you Bartarino." He said as there was a huge sand like hand that reached in and pulled us out.

"What was that about?" Gina asked.

"Nothing!"

"Aden, stop! I'm tired of not knowing, and being spoken around. What was that about?"

"These things are over your head. Do you want to get left behind?" I yelled, "Let's go."

"What's Nirew?" Gina asked.

"No questions just walk." I said. Gina followed behind me as I walked out of the gates and Dar and Kilen appeared.

"So much for being in good with these things." I snapped.

"My king Aden, we didn't know Prince Griven was at the gates this daybreak." Kilen said.

"Yes that was very disappointing. Doesn't seem like much of a kinship." I walked faster with every step.

"Hey Aden! I don't know what your problem is, but don't be rude to them. It's them putting their life on the line for us." Gina said.

"Imperative information, it's for your safety. I don't need them. I've been doing pretty well on my own until you came around or haven't you noticed yet?" I turned towards her.

"Really, King Aden! Please forgive me. Should I bow to you now? Should I thank you? Do you want me to grovel at your feet?" Gina stood still.

"Don't do that."

"Don't do what? You are a king. Which you just forgot to mention."

"I am not a king. I told you everything that's happening was a curse. I didn't ask for it. So don't you dare be condescending! I yelled "Now let's go."

"You are such a jerk Aden." Gina said walking pass me.

"I don't owe you anything. Not an excuse, nothing! You've gotten yourself in this." I walked behind her.

"I'll keep that on file. Just get me to the cure for my friend, and we never have to be around each other anymore." Gina said

"Hey!" I noticed myself losing control of the situation because she was good with manipulating the conversation with her attitude, and I walked up to her, "Turn around, when I'm talking to you." I yelled.

"I am not your servant or your slave. I don't have to listen or talk to you." Gina fired back.

"Enough!" Dar said. "Sorry my king, but we must move, for it will be daybreak soon."

"Fine!" I said.

"Fine." Gina walked on.

We walked in silence. I hated that. Gina was really good at being quiet. I expected her to at least curse me in her thoughts, but she was good at holding everything together. She wouldn't even look my way. We had stopped for a break from walking. Gina sat in a dress she had worn ever since we left Queen Patano, she was shivering. You can tell our journey has taking its effect on it with all the tears and dirt.

"Give her this." I said handing Dar my cloak.

"I think its best if you give it to her. You seem to have feelings for her my king." Dar said.

"I'm not your king. I can't have these feelings. I have one purpose here and so does she." I whispered.

"You will find that you are our king, in time. You can't stop feelings that arrive. You must deal with them, don't hide them. Your father wouldn't have like you to fight your feelings he would've want you to own them." Dar said.

"You know what I must do. If I choose anyone. You know the promise I made him when I was in young eras." I said.

"A promise from a young one, changes with time. That comes with every promise that was made. You will always grow and learn. That is maybe why promises were asked of you." Dar said. "This may solely be a matter to consult with your advisors."

"Just take her the cloak." I said and Dar walked away. I walked the cloak over to Gina and I starred at her as she hesitated to take it, but she did and she noticed the steam surround her hands as she took the cloak in. I remove my eyes from her, and walked away. She wrapped it around her. Kilen appeared with wood and sat them in the middle of the ground.

"Aden, the wood." Kilen said. I walked over to the sticks, looking straight towards Gina, gazing in her brown eyes. I reached my hands over them, and lit them. She looked at me as if she felt the way I felt; lost and confused. Her heart pounding in her chest, and she just looked away. I walked back to a spot further away, and sat. What do I do next father? I looked to the sky.

Chapter 7: The King of Berut Mountains

The sun has risen and we traveled far from the sands of Tanas Gates. During our travel to Aden's home we now enter the main village of the Berut Mountains. This was a small community of creatures. They lived in valleys and seem to struggle with survival. You can see starvation within them all and you can tell by the clothes they wore many of them had nothing. Their clothes were torn and dirty. The mountains surrounding the valley were so high it appeared as if it was night. The sun shined in a different direction. It was foggy and gloomy.

The creatures were all shapes and sizes. They had children of different colors, and breeds. Women and men, old and young; you couldn't tell what they were because most looked like they had defects. They saw us walking down the pavement, some took their children into the homes and locked the doors, while others gossiped. Although I couldn't understand it, Aden did. He had covered his face. Dar pushed one creature away from me, whom tried to grab me and he stood close by me. Kilen was posted in front of Aden. There were creatures chained to poles hammering metal of some sort. The cruelty that had been placed upon these creatures was tormenting to the gut. There were some who were chained to buildings, I'm guessing because they had committed crimes. They hung in grief, looking as if they were begging for freedom.

As we walked through this village we came upon a giant mountain. We had approached stone steps that were creatively made on the side of the mountain. Each stone seemed to be designed according to one's specific taste. They remind me of a bottom slay. We found Guards standing protectively in front of the steps. They growled like defensive dogs, until Aden showed his face. They all bowed and backed away. Kilen glided up the steps and Aden. This was the first time I saw him do that. Dar glided as well. I as much as I could ran behind them. After a long journey up the steps, we reached the top. A palace set ahead of us. When the guards in front of the palace noticed us they opened huge doors. We heard a boisterous voice, "King Aden, I had received word you were on the travel here."

Mockingly spoke a big man who sat on a throne with two women strapped in collars and chains around their neck. They sat next to the throne like animals. Hair flowing down their backs and they were laced with revealing silk clothing. It was as if it's some kind of male adult dream he was living out in reality.

"King Griven, I come to pass through the Mountains to reach my home land." Aden said.

"Are you telling me or asking, young Aden?" The king responded.

"I am asking to pass through your village, without a struggle from you or from your guards." Aden watched the guards circle us.

"A king demands not asks. Oh you have a lot to learn. Your father would be very disappointed." King Griven said.

"This is no manner about my father." Aden said.

"Your father will not rise from the ashes and put me in my place." Aden stepped forward, but Dar held him back. "You were always a spoiled child. Your father was always so protective over little Prince Aden. I feel pleasure for you as much as I liked your father." King Griven chuckled "And I liked your father as much as I could lift my right arm, and I can't lift it high." He gestured his arm up, and it fell immediately to the arm of his chair as he chuckled.

"That's enough." Aden became flustered

"Why does your Being not have a leash?" King Griven asked.

"Excuse me." I said.

"This is a civil Being." Aden snapped his head back at me. His eyes commanded that I shut up.

"I keep these skins on a leash, so no other may take them. They are my catch, so I keep them." King Griven said. "Is she your catch Aden?"

"No." Aden said undoubtedly still angered about the comments about his father.

"Dar, is she your catch?" King Griven asked.

"No, King Griven. She will be no threat to you or anyone else." Dar said.

"Kilen, is she yours?"

"No. But I give you my word, she poses no threat." Kilen said

"You give me your word." King Griven laughed "If she is no one's catch, and she poses no irrelevant threat, I shall add her to my collection." Griven snapped his fingers and one of his guards grabbed me.

"Let me go." One of Griven guards grabbed me as I screamed and kicked. It was a tall and ugly creature with thick flaky, spiky skin. Aden put his arm out.

"She is my keep." Aden said "Unhand her, or a wisp of a millisecond you will become ashes."

I liked those words that came out of his mouth. They felt real. It really felt like he meant that I was his keep. My attraction for him had grown over these past days. I saw the way he pretended not to watch me, when he wanted to say things, and didn't say them. There was a connection he didn't want to put them together. I don't even know how it would work, he couldn't touch me. Would he ever be able touch me? Would I burn to make it possible? For him, at this moment I would.

"You said that she wasn't; so let's say she's mine if you want to make it out of here alive." King Griven had spoken in a mischievous tone.

"Why is it that a king dream's to tests another king?" Aden smiled.

"You won't make it out alive, my would be king." King Griven said.

Aden hands lit up and Kilen circled around the guards making the dust on the floor rise like smoke. The dust was thick, I couldn't see a thing. I noticed Dar heavy breath flew pass my ears, and I heard Aden grunts, I was dropped on the floor. There was dead silence, until the smoke settled the guards lay on the floor as the king clapped and smiled. Aden stood in front of me, and Dar to the left and Kilen to my right. "Excellent. You have up kept your father's skills even in that Beings world. But tell me, how do you expect to handle them? King Griven asked pointing to an army full of creatures standing at the front and back exit.

"I want no coil with your men. I want to get through these mountains. The more intense that you make this, it will make it hard for me to just wound them." Aden said.

King Griven chuckled, "I will oblige you this once because your homecoming will seem to be deathly."

"Let them through." We walked towards the exit on the opposite side of the castle, and before we exited, "Be sure to give good greetings to Nirew." King Griven stare was so cold, at Aden. "Do not let that one out of your sight at all." he laughed.

We walked down another flight of steps as King Griven guards opened the stone doors; a rush of bright lights hit us like in the Nitzer. We stepped into what seem to be the dead of winter. The mountains were covered with snow. It seems their climate changes from warm, cold to freezing cold, with snow in a blink of an eye, but through all these oddities of events, I was more curious of this Nirew. Why does everyone say that name? What did it mean? I want to know, but Aden looked angry. He seems to be out of it. He stared straight ahead.

"Aden..." I said as he looked straight ahead.

"What?" He shook his head out of a day dream.

"What is Nirew?" I asked.

"Nirew is not a what. It's who?" He looked over hesitating to go further into the conversation. "In addition to what's in your mind, it's a delicate situation... Be careful what you ask you may get the answers to what you so desperately seek." Aden said and turned away from me. I said nothing. He seemed so distance. We hadn't really spoken after our big blow up. He wouldn't look my way or even speak to me. I must admit, we both were a little heated, but his anger goes deep. It's like a force field, once you press a button with him, it's hard to undo- what is done. We walked and walked, everyone was silent.

"Aden thank you." I said.

"For what?" He asked climbing up a steep snowy hill, in an instant everything was covered with snow, and cold. The mountains were a beautiful color, a gray and mahogany mixture of some sort. I could see the distance between us and another set of mountains. The air in the mountains was fresh, thin, and they were tall and covered from top to bottom with the snow. The briskly freezing wind blew sometimes knocking snow around on us, which made me colder. I would really love to be in a nice steaming hot room, to warm up.

"You saved me from a leash." I smirked trying to ease the tension, but it went nowhere. I tried keeping myself warm in this dress I had on. I wrapped my arms around me for warmth, following Aden and the others on this travel through the snowy conditions.

Aden took off his cloak and put it on top of my shoulders. It was so warm, I loved it. But it also was so heavy to carry. Aden wasn't a little guy at all. This cloak felt like it weighed two-thousand pounds.

"We have not that far to go to the next rest." Kilen said.

"Dar carry on ahead." Aden said and Dar positioned himself in the front with Kilen.

"I wish I knew how Maggie is doing." I said.

"My father advisor may have a way to look in on her." Aden said.

"I'm sorry for my behavior, through a lot of this."

"Don't…" Aden contest.

"Don't what? Why won't you let me in.? You're so distant with me."

"I can't." Aden said.

"Why can't you?"

"Remember I can read your mind."

"I know." I said.

"First, it wouldn't work. I can't touch you. I can never touch you. Second, it's a price for me to pay returning to Nexima. Lastly and definitely not least, I can't keep a Being in this world unless you… would be subjected to a leash." Aden stopped as I abruptly stood in his path.

"What?" I faced him.

"Beings are like dogs in my world."

"Well you're a king, change that rule." I said.

"I can't and time will prove that it's needed." Aden said.

"What! Why?"

"Aren't you here to save your friend? Our growing feelings don't matter. You still have to leave."

"I keep trying to fight this attraction with you, but I can't. You're so difficult." I said.

"My difficulties are difficult." Aden said.

"I like difficult, because I happen to be the same way."

"It would never work."

"You're afraid to give anything a chance, aren't you?"

"And you are young and naïve to believe that all you envision could come true." His volume increased.

"There's something you're not telling me." Aden looked away. "Aden! Whatever is further ahead you need to speak to me."

"Nirew is a princess I was raised with. I promised my father, I would marry her to keep unity in my village." Aden said looking away, and then he looked into my eyes.

"Wow! I never saw that coming!" It hit me like a ton of rocks and I stood in silence and wanted to sit down... "It's okay. I'm sorry." I said walking off.

"Gina!" Aden said as Dar and Kilen turned towards me, and stood in my path, I turned towards Aden.

"No. Let's just go. I think I agree I asked more than I wanted to know." We walked again, but I tried to walk faster so I wouldn't cry.

****

As we walked through the snowy mountains I listened to Gina fill her mind with thoughts to prepare her for the encounters ahead. We approached a stone door that Dar, Kilen and I had to move with all our might. As we entered into a deep cave, the door shut behind us. It became pitch black dark, but a light shined brightly ahead. As we approached it became brighter, like the light was meeting us half way. We heard a familiar voice.

"How did we arrive here before you?" Queen Patano asked stepping into our view holding an antique lantern that had literature etched out on its cover.

"We ran into some trouble." I said.

"Was it the always ambitious Griven's?" Lilar said alongside Queen Patano.

"You knew that they were occupying around the gates and mountains." I asked.

"Aden, If you should remember, King Griven occupies that land since your father ruled." Queen Patano said.

There was no conversation, but between Queen Patano and I. Dar was quiet, Kilen said nothing like always, and Gina had definitely silenced. She even fights hard to silence her thoughts. She was so ambitiously silent it distracted me from my abilities, and I couldn't hear her heart beat anymore. That was something I longed to hear every day. As we walked we suddenly came upon a castle built inside the snowy mountains. This castle was built exclusively for my father through his travel to maintain peace. I vaguely remember being here through my childhood. We entered the castle and Gina was shown to a room reserved for her as hours passed she didn't come out. I walked to her door, and stood by it just to smell her scent. I don't know why, but it comes to comfort me. I've become so emotionally distracted from Gina's vacancy it feels me with similar feelings of my life without my mother and father. Gina and I have known each other for so little time, but we both have come to a place where we have affected each other lives forever.

"Even if you knocked my king, she would not open it." Queen Patano said.

"It was not my intent to knock." I said walking away from the door.

"You two breed an unspeakable bond."

"We don't."

"If you don't, why stand outside her door?"

"Her protection is my responsibility. And it doesn't help to speak of this fictional unspeakable bond." I stopped in front of Queen Patano.

"My king, your elder council can be swayed to the king wishes." Queen Patano said.

"Queen Patano, if my memory serves me well, my father said, you were a great advisor to my mother, and I remember you telling me that my mother's only wish ask of me, was to be a great son to my father. So when it's my choice to return home. What would you have me do? I made my father a promise." I walked away as Queen Patano followed.

"My king I'm not one of your chosen advisors, so with respect, it's not my place to give thoughts that may alter your path."

"Queen Patano you've been guiding me through the way back to Sawdawa, wouldn't that make you my advisor?" I stopped once more. Looking the Queen in her eyes and I was patiently awaiting an answer.

"My king, it's a personal command from King Ndea and Queen Fliparia Masa Bartarino in some misfortune of any kind that may cause your absence upon their land, which I look over all Sawdawa.

My home is Congo Plains and if it is your wish to return to Sawdawa to be king, Congo Plains is where I would reside. But if it gives any sentiments, all that's in your mind that you may characterize as foolish thoughts, and occurring feelings leading to your poor broken heart. You may even break your promise. Even still you will experience all that you fight against. Just as you crave once again you will hear her heartbeat and out of all this you might even stop using your gifts as a curse. You were consecrated by your parent's blood. My highest." Queen Patano said gliding away.

I laid that sunset trying to sleep. Queen Patano words ran through my head over and over again. I could hear it. Her heart beat. It was close. I raised myself from my bed, and I walked through the hallways, until I reached a room with large windows, and there with the wind whistling, blowing through her hair stood Gina. Her gown was long and a pale Yellow. It swayed side to side. "Why are you here?" Gina asked without looking back.

"I felt the air." I said as her heartbeat slowly.

"It was a mistake to come here. Even trying with you, it was all a mistake." Gina said. I said nothing. It was relaxing to hear her say something. I eased my way next to her.

"How did you know it was me?"

"I felt you." She smiled. "The same way I always do." I still said nothing. I watched her look out of the window.

"Maggie will be okay."

"You're reading my thoughts again Aden." She smiled.

"I'm sorry, I didn't mean too." She turned toward me.

"We've never been this close."

"I know." I tried to back away but, I was being pulled towards her. We were like magnets.

"Your eyes, they are red." Gina said "Such a deep color for a serious person."

"I can't help that I'm what you call so serious all the time." I said.

"You could if you tried."

"We will be in my father's land tomorrow. You can try to get in contact with Maggie then."

"Do you think she's better?" Gina asked as she turned back to the window.

"I don't know." There was a gap of silence and then she glanced at me. Her eyes were beautiful and brown.

"What would happen if..."

"If what?" she turned towards me, moving close, "You would get hurt." I backed away.

"Try to touch me." She said.

"I don't want to hurt you." I balled my hands into fists, to stop myself from touching her. She tilted her head moving close to mine. Her smell was enticing, and the way her breath felt against my skin made my hands uncontrollable, they reached for her face, the sound of her heart beating made me move more towards her. With every beat I stepped closer. I had no power, no resistance. I wanted her. "I can't." I said stepping back from her, trying to fight it.

"It's fine." She said as she turned to walk away, but I didn't want her to leave.

"No." I said. She stopped and turned towards me. I looked in her eyes, she felt safe, and she had no worries, she trusted me, which made me reach my hands out towards her, I hesitated to touch her. As my hands extended out in mid-air, she stared at them as she leaned in closer. I didn't know what to do. She hesitated to touch me, but she ran her hands across my arms and she looked at me. Nothing happened. I stared in her eyes; she stood on her toes, gently slid her lips against mine. It seemed like microseconds, the more pressure she applied, I responded the same. I instantly felt my hands drop upon her waist. I didn't want to let her go. She wanted this as much as I did. I heard it in her thoughts. Her heart relaxed. I felt mine speed up. Everything was fine for brief seconds; her arms went up around my neck. Our hearts were in sync together; I ran my fingers through her hair, pulling her lips closer to mine.

I didn't want to fight this feeling anymore. Maybe everyone was wrong. I was touching her. Her lips were as soft as I imagined. Her hands slid up towards my face. She felt my scars as if they weren't there. This magical moment took over us for a few seconds. Nature took its course, my body ignited for a split second burning her lips. She screamed and my hands burned her waist as I pushed her away.

"I'm sorry." I said.

"It's okay."

"I shouldn't have done that." I could barely breathe. I exhaled and inhaled fast.

"It's fine. Aden I'm okay."

"No! I lost control. I'm sorry." I said it was clear I step out of my element and she was controlling this situation.

"It's ok, she moved closer. I'm fine." She reached for me again and I stepped away looking at her waist and lips that were bruised.

"I'll send Queen Patano in with something to heal your skin." I glided out of the room.

"Aden." She yelled for me, but I kept going.

■■
****

Moments had passed as I walked around looking for Aden, but I couldn't find him. I wanted to let him know I was fine. Even though when I licked my lips or pressed them together, the pain felt a little like burning them with an iron. He seemed paranoid, and guilty. I entered the room I was staying in, and laid in the bed. Was I wrong for what happened? Did I make him break rules he shouldn't have? Now I felt guilty, I'm here for one reason, and I got emotionally attached to this strange guy Aden. If Maggie were here she would smack me, and tell me to get on track. I miss her so much. I cannot imagine what she's going through. There was a knock at the door.

"Come in?" I said.

"It's your friend Being." Queen Patano said.

"What's wrong?" I sat up.

"She's in grave danger." Queen Patano said. I never notice that her skin sagged underneath her yellow eyes.

"What's wrong with her?"

"Come!" Queen Patano walked out of the room. I followed her to a well-lit room, where Dar, Kilen, Lilar, and Aden stood looking down to the floor, making no eye contact.

"What's going on?" I asked and saw an image big in the middle of the floor.

"There is a message." Aden said.

"What message?" I asked.

"Don't panic, for what's going to happen. Keep your eyes open. There's a message from Ponchopalapare." Queen Patano turns and walked towards me her eyes glow a yellow brighter than before. The skin around her eyes sagged more. "Being this is the way we transfer messages through our world. Look into my eyes he cannot harm you." Queen Patano said as she held my arms, as I looked in her eyes and a split second a beam of light leaves from her eyes to my eyes. I was looking into a dark room with Maggie stretched out in thin air. The creature alongside her, was uglier than the she-ads I've seen. He was tall, hands as big as elephant's feet. He had no eyes and a huge nose.

"Maggie." I screamed. The beast turned towards me.

"My message is for King Aden Bartarino. Not for a Being from the other world. But if Queen Patano has given you these eyes, then you must have close counsel with our young Aden. So the King Bartarino for the filthy being." Ponchopalapare said as he reaches his hands for me as the bright light appears and I was once again with Aden, Queen Patano, and the others.

"Where is she?" I cried.

"We have no knowledge where he's keeping her." Queen Patano said as the skins around her eyes tighten.

"We need to leave this rest. Our eyes into his eyes give him eyes into our eyes. He has located us." Dar said.

"Someone needs to do something." I cried.

"Kilen we need to leave now." Queen Patano said.

"Yes my Queen." Kilen said.

"Aden, you have to do something." I said, but he didn't respond. "Aden please, promise me you will get her back." Tears ran down my cheeks like rain drops.

"It's my life's promise." He said looking at me with an almost guilty look. The floor started shaking; there were hard pounding and beating against the castle. There were sounds of growls, and howls outside the walls.

"They're here." Dar yelled.

"Everyone take your places, we have to get out of here." Aden said.

"There are two Nitzers ready to take off on the lower caves. But we would have to leave Dar behind." Lilar said.

"No." I said.

"Gina, It is my destiny. You can't fight what's meant to happen." Dar said.

"Dar." I cried.

"Go get into the Nitzer." Kilen said. Lilar lead us down into the lower end of the castle deep inside the cave where two giant oval shaped bright lights shined. Aden and Kilen walks up to one, and Queen Patano, and Lilar to another. They touched the lights with three fingers, the index, ring, and pinky fingers. The lights shut off, showing a black shiny marble like quality. The doors opened, showing seating, and transportation technology inside.

"Quickly get in Gina." Aden said. We all got into the oval shaped cars, which people on earth would think of them like Jetson cars. The middle part of the car had a bubbling form, slowly the bubbles stacked up one by one that formed wind panels to withstand and fly through the air. As we sat in the car, the monitors in the car showed every inch of outside the Nitzer, left, right, back ground. The monitors calculated every step around the Nitzer. As the Nitzer moved as a Lexus operates their park it yourself technology I notice smoke rising from the ground as the Nitzer compresses off the ground. With a powerful jet like movement we flew in the air. I noticed looking out of the window we were coming upon a mountain wall fast and it didn't seem like Aden would make a turn.

"Aden! Do you see that wall?" I asked, "oh, oh my...." I screamed covering my eyes. After noticing that we should have hit the wall by now, I opened my eyes remembering that this was a alien ship and we flew through the rest walls. Once we cleared, a She-ad jumped on the Nitzer we were in. The She-ad raised his arm with a hammer and before he could attack the windshield an arrow hits his chest, Aden flipped the car over and the She-ad flew off. I looked back and seen the arrow came from Dar who was raising his hand to us. As we go further ahead I looked back and realized he gave his life for us. Our way to Aden's village wouldn't be as smooth as I hoped. Everyone was taking a huge risk for me, and my safety. I was angry that I had caused so much trouble, trying to be a friend to someone who was doing well on his own. I wonder if this was my destiny as I hear Dar voice inside my head saying, "It's my destiny I can't fight what's meant to be."

Chapter 8: Congo Plains

Congo Plains was the last stop on my journey to my homeland. This is Queen Patano's land. Every specie under her ruling has unmerciful allegiance to my father. Before we can enter her kingdom, we must meet up with her royal guards to lead her back into her castle. This is for protection for not only their queen, but for their soon to be king. I had made a promise to Gina that I would save her friend. Was it possible? Was I willing? For her, a Being I tried to care nothing about. That kiss, was like none other. Nothing could top that feeling I felt when I wrapped my arms around Gina. I felt culpable. My allegiance was to Nirew, but Gina's where my heart seemed to be headed towards. Could it be that I'm ready to feel something for someone? But would it have been Nirew if I were home? I didn't even know my heart could beat like this. Nirew is a princess from my world, and she will marry someone of her families choosing. She would hold firm to the choosing of her new life unless there was a reason for her to change. She knew everything about me. Me, love a Being… is that what was happening? Would I forsake the dying wishes of my father? Is this what it means to befriend someone? I had to distance myself from these thoughts.

"There is another rest ahead my king, ten scales to your right. Where Queen Patano guards will join us and lead us to her Kingdom." Kilen spoke through the speakers in the Nitzer.

"I see it now." As I prepare to land I looked at Gina sleeping on the passenger side of the Nitzer. It had been hours of traveling to Congo Plains. I landed as gently as possible. I took off my cloak and laid it on top of her. She twitched from the steam coming from it, but you could tell she appreciated it as she pulled it tightly up to her face. I got out of the Nitzer, and closed the door. I looked back and Gina hadn't awakened.

"King Aden, Queen Patano. We have awaited your arrival." Ballajamen said one of Queen Patano trusted guards stood. One of Queen Patano guards came before me and knelt.

"My king, I'm over joyed, the tales of your return are true, and my name is Fullupian." As he spoke I grew uncomfortable.

"Please rise." I looked around, to the far deep of the forest; I observed Skins kneeling as if they were embracing the emotion of Fullupian.

"My king, your return has been spoken through every stem of the trees." Queen Patano said, "Royal embrace will never end for you."

"My return is only for the inconvenient Being." I said.

"For whatever purpose of your return, you have awakened our world. Follow me." Queen Patano said.

"Fullupian, stand aside the Nitzer. Keep watch. Do not shed respect of this Being as you will respect me. This Being is in my care." I said as I followed Queen Patano inside the forest as we walk a tall tree with branches filled with hair-like leaves burst opened. I noticed the skins in the far distance, their stare with ambitious eyes then the tree began to move allowing a doorway inside Queen Patano walks in and I followed. As Queen Patano, myself, Kilen, and Lilar stepped in, without looking back I heard the tree slapped together shutting close with a loud smack. We observed a giant room in twenty full armed guards standing waiting.

"Teteman step forward." Kilen said, a seven foot tall mountain skin, swords man stepped up. Mountain Skins were rare creatures in my world. They were tall, and their skin resembled the mountain rocks, and is tough to penetrate through. They were created from the tricks of sand demons. Never to know they could make judgments of their own, they separated from their creators.

"My king I have arrived with your two special guards from Sawdawa." Teteman said with a deep ghastly voice.

"Sanduwe and Parfar, Step forward," I asked. The two guards stepped forward, one Phantom that resembles Kilen and a cross breed like I, mixed sand creature and phantom.

"Here at your command my king," They speak in unison and bow.

"My old friends, I've kept an eye on you from a far, and the journey I must take, I will need your expertise." I said. "Our training as young ones, have grown in resemblance."

"We are over joy of your return my king," Parfar spoke.

"It is of great pleasure to be on the battlefield with you." Sanduwe said.

"Arm yourself, and lead us into my palace." Queen Patano said as I watched them grab and load their holsters with weapons. Suddenly I hear a yell. "We are under attack." Ballajamen yelled.

"Gina." I glided through the trees walls. There were skins surrounding the Nitzers. I move swiftly, where the Skins were trying to break through the Nitzer. Gina awakened and screamed. Suddenly the Skins ripped unmercifully bleeding as they turned from Skins to She-ads. I looked at Queen Patano, whom looked just as surprised as I did to observe She-ads with ability to makes themselves as Skins. One of them strong and tall turns from banging on the Nitzer, looking towards me.

"King Aden we have come for you, give up and we won't feed on her bones." A She-ad spoke with a grizzly smirk. As the She-ads stood at attention I glided quickly over towards him, grabbing his neck. My hands began to heat up, he smiles and with great strength he grabs my neck and throws me into a tree. Kilen, Sanduwe, Parfar, and other guards leap into battle. The She-ads jumps over as I stood, he grabs my neck and raise me.

"You haven't learned yet, runaway king. So I have been sent for quick teaching and with the last glimpse of your life, you shall remember me." He said. He lifted me in the air as I wrapped my hands around his wrist. While his hands smoked, but it didn't seem to bother him. The heat from my body didn't faze him. I swung, and he threw me against the mountain. I kicked him off me.

"My king." Kilen threw me an emerald dagger, but the creature knocked it down. Kilen glided over and stabbed the creature with the blade. There's a war going on. It was too many of the She-ads and a battle forming.

"Battle yourself to the Nitzers." I yelled to everyone. I battled myself back to Gina inside the Nitzer. I got inside and as we pulled off. I watched the creature struggle to rise with Kilen's blade in him.

"King Aden, Sanduwe and Parfar were left in the battle." Teteman said through a transmitter.

"I gave direct orders." I said.

"They asked to be left behind to investigate the She-ads lair that's been discovered not too far away from the rest." Lilar said.

"I ordered everyone to leave. Turn back." I said.

"No, they are trained soldiers my king. Their life is battle, that's the reasons for their existence, and their journey is the honorable way." Queen Patano said.

****

The ride was filled with silence and Aden would show frustration and hit the steering wheel. Everything was happening all at once, all my feelings for Aden, Maggie being held hostage, these thoughts of being a witness to whom he truly loved once we arrive to his home. I envisioned Maggie dying, and Aden getting married. It all was so frustrating. He wouldn't talk.

"Aden, are you okay?" I asked reaching for him.

"Don't! I'm fine." He snapped.

"I'm sorry…"

"No need to apologize." Aden cut me off.

It bothered me that this is his life. My existence and his existence depended on him being alone. He hated that I had even been around, he didn't say it, and just because of me this was happening. No one likes losing people. Not the people you care most about. We arrived in front of the palace doors. As we exited the Nitzers, the village was very welcoming to Aden and his comrades. This was in deed, Queen Patano homeland because it was made up of two legged four arm creatures such as Queen Patano. The palace sat at the end of the road which was smooth, no rocks no bumps. It was a perfectly made road. I looked at the front of her palace, it was made in her image. The top floor was her head and hair flowing to her legs. This was a beautiful palace if I had to say so myself. Gold as if to reflect the riches she has. There were all sorts of exotic flowers in front next to a gushing waterfall. Walking up the stone steps I really had to stretch my legs. They were not made for a human to walk up. When reaching the top, I was out of breath.

"Come with me Being. We must talk." Queen Patano said. I looked at Aden watching us walk away. You could tell looking at Queen Patano garment and looking at her home, she loved silks and porcelain. We walked into this beautifully design room, she sat on plush pillows designed in different styles, and they looked to be designed with arm rests the resembled antlers. "My servants will escort you to your quarters. Aden will need this time to adjust to the coming moments in his life."

"I wasn't going anywhere near him." I fidgeted with my hands. Queen Patano laughed.

"For the ones in your atmosphere, you two are the biggest catastrophe, I may have ever seen in my two-thousand eras."

"What does that mean?" I asked.

"My king has grown fond of you." She drank from a cup that her servant had given to her."

"From my understanding Aden is meant for this Nirew, or whatever her name is."

"Don't trout around the life of this moment. You two must put a period on your interaction." Queen Patano said.

"I'm not trying to make him break a promise he made to his dying father. Plus, I'm an outlaw here."

"As I know, you hear his heartbeat, as he hears yours."

"What does that mean?"

"It means dear one, you know his feelings and he knows yours. You two avoid it much."

"Aden lives by promises and does what he wants at the same time. Just as he says I'm here to save my friend."

"You both are young. These moments bring wisdom, and you know not wisdom when you hear it." Queen Patano said.

"I'm seeing in this world he has his life mapped out for him."

"But it is you that is changing the map that you speak of. You both shall halt and speak after his meditation. My servant here," Queen Patano said pointing to a Skin alongside of her, "She will take you to your quarters. You two shall discuss all, you two must find answers." She said. I exited her lavish quarters. I walked around Queen Patano's home, it was more beautiful than the rest she had. It was full of so many exotic colors and paintings she had clay statues made in her likeness, wrapped in gold. The servant seemed to glide across the floors, and she glanced back watching me as if I were up to something. Her eyes were deep into her face and black. She stood taller than I. Her hair flowed in a high ponytail. Her nails had come out of her skin as if she would attack me as she walked. I walked far from her. As I followed, I passed a room hearing grunts, I saw the door was cracked, my eyes quickly recognized the person inside, and it was Aden. I stopped following Queen Patano's servant. Aden was hitting a vertical, rectangular padded balloon. Every time he hit the bag, it would come towards him with more force, and directed it attacked towards him. His hair was long and wet from sweat; he swung at the balloon shirtless. I could see his battle scars from in his seclusion He put so much energy into every move he made.

"You may enter if you like." Aden said without turning around.

"Oh, I'm sorry! I don't want to bother you." I said turning away.

"Come on. My meditation has eased my mind." I turned back and entered the room. I stepped down onto the bamboo floors. The room was exquisite. It had somewhat of an Asian feel to it. Aden had walked over to a porcelain table with two porcelain glasses and a mug. He sat down in a chair identical to the table. "Sit over here, I won't bite." He smiled that smile that made me like him even more.

"I didn't know you had a fitness routine." I said.

"No, I just made that thing today. Pieces of your world work here." Aden said, "We have a lot of your home things. We have been known to enjoy things in this world."

"Oh."

"I'm kidding. We have most of Earth things. Some of us lived there long enough to know how to update this world." He laughed taking tape from around his hands and I smiled.

"You have a beautiful smile." He said staring at me.

"Thank you." I continued to smile and thought about how sexy he was with his shirt off. I watched the sweat drip down, and parts of me wanted to just feel it.

"Ah, thank you. Didn't know you like topless creatures." He said reading my mind.

"Aden, you heard that." I shielded my face. "I'm sorry; I forgot my thoughts aren't mine when you're around.

"They are yours. I just wanted to make you blush."

"Do you want to speak about the huge promises that await you coming back?" I asked and he stopped smiling.

"It's just certain things, I do not wish to discuss with you."

"Why? I've been nice haven't I?"

"I don't want you to declare me as a bad person. Alone with getting the remedy for Maggie, the knowledge arises of my father death. That breeds another mission to kill my fathers' killer." He stood up and walked towards a window and I followed.

"You're not a bad person, you want revenge. I understand that."

"Revenge! Is that what you would do?" Aden asked

"My father left me; I don't know where he is." I leaned against the wall.

"What about your mother?" He asked sincerely.

"She put me out when I was twenty. She told me there was a world I needed to explore, and that I didn't need her anymore."

"That's harsh, with a little dose of insight." Aden said

"That's my life, in a nut shell. What about your mother?" I asked.

"I never met her. I heard tales and my father told me stories of her. She left me when I was young."

"Wow! We have more in common than I thought." I said, and he stared at me.

"I didn't want to hurt you that night, you know?" He said.

"You didn't. It was just a little pain… I enjoyed the kiss. If I could do it again, I would."

"You would? Even after what happened?"

"Yes." I said, and he looked at me with curious eyes.

"You're a big risk taker, aren't you?" Aden asked

"I have one life to live; I want to live it to the fullest." He stood in front of me.

"Could you live with me not touching you, every day until you died?" Aden asked

"It would take getting used to. But I could if I tried." I replied nervously being so close to him. My eyes fluttered looking from his lips to his eyes.

"It would honestly kill me. It's killing me now, not to touch you. This is not a life for anyone, not to have contact with the one you love." Aden said moving towards me examining my eyes.

"You love?" I was curious of his words. And he stared. I could barely breathe at a normal pace because of the distance of his body from mine; I blinked erratically staring into his eyes. I felt calm and at ease while I moved my face closer to his, closing my eyes at the temperature of his breath on my lips.

He moved closer as both his hands were on the wall behind me. His lips were inches from mine and his eyes were closed. Aden was telling himself not to do it. I wanted him to so bad. It was like my body was prepared as I stood on my tiptoes. His right hand reached for my neck, but it too stopped in its place. I felt the warmth from afar. He was pleading to himself under his breath. He opened his eyes, and I paused, we again stared at each other and we both moved away. "This would be a good time to pull away. Good night." I walked out of the room.

"Gina." He yelled "Gina."

****

Queen Patano entered her study room where I sat. She wanted me to speak; I remember the look on her face. She makes it when she wants me to spill my guts. This time I refrain, she would have to talk. But she didn't. Was her silence one lesson she must teach me from my mother.

"I'm befuddled Queen Patano." I said.

"About?" she responded.

"These emotions I'm having. I've grown fond of Gina…no it's more than that."

"You love her."Queen Patano said.

"I have yet to confirm if that's the meaning of these feelings."

"From my judgment, it's what you feel King Aden. When you can never describe the way you feel for another, its love."

"How can I love her when I'm bond to another?"

"That's bond by your legacy not your heart. Unconsciously it seems Gina has spoken for your heart."

"I could never touch her." I walked around her study, "I hurt her when we kissed. A Being was never meant to join with my kind. What is wrong with me?" I hit the table frustrated.

"There's immeasurable possibilities, but first you must drop your guard from taking your proper place upon the throne and seek the knowledge of your counsel." Queen Patano said.

"They are nothing alike, one is young and inexperienced, and the other has been very loyal."

"I can never speak judgment on your choice on your Queen. Nirew has been patiently waiting, but also Gina and you have built a bond for the future of battle worlds."

"This legacy of my father has placed a curse upon the life I wish to lead." I said.

"This curse you speak of is what stands between the Beings world and our world colliding and bring death to many houses. We have barely protected this world without the guiding of you and your kingdom. You will find the situation as your being friends would say a moment away from a hundred pound stone being dropped through a sheet of paper."

"I am not a king." Aden said.

"I fear the world if you are not." Queen Patano said. "Good sunset." She walked out of the room.

"Good sunset." I said. It was like Patano only came around when she felt vibrations with one's mind. She is like an extension of my mother. It seems to be the only mother I've known. I believe in everything she says. I have strong feelings for Gina, but I made a promise to my father. I grow close to breaking that promise, because of these feelings for Gina and because of my absence; my feelings are fading for Nirew. How do I tell Gina my feelings? I also feel that I shouldn't, because if I foresaw no matter what, I must join with Nirew. In our order, in our race of people we never broke promises. We never gave our word, and backed out of it. I have foreseen no way out of this and when we were to come rescue Maggie that was it. I have to get rid of these feelings I have, immediately.

Chapter 9: Aden's fortress

I was having mixed sentiments and didn't know if I wanted to honor my father wishes, or just do what I was feeling. Never have I disobeyed my father since I've lived, but this was one of the times I strongly consider it. Encountering Gina changed me; I would be lying if I said it didn't. Nirew was another I didn't want to disappoint. She has been waiting eras for me to come home; she has waited all this time to join with me. It has grown truthfully that she seeks no other. We have been traveling moments to my homeland and the silence between Gina and I in this tank was deafening. Her eyes were red from exhaustion. She has unending thoughts of Maggie, but she never talked about her. She was sad today. Her references gave no thought of me, it could be her way of letting me know how angry she was, and maybe that's what I wanted. I considered it. She even called me a jerk, a few times. It somewhat disappointed me. But she was right to feel that.

"Gina, can we talk?" I asked her.

"Okay." Gina said as she straightens herself in the seat.

"I must apologize."

"For what?" She looked at me.

"I should have done more to stop your emerging to our world. As soon as you saw a glimpse of me, I should've departed." I said.

"No one needs to live a life alone like that." She said avoided my eyes.

"You should be able to conceive now that my alone is safe."

"Well, I guess we both have to consider what we regret, and the feelings festering between us."

"Regret! I never…"

"Wow!" She looked out of the window.

"Is this where you live?" The conversation had become stagnant to what Gina was seeing.

"Yes, welcome to Sawdawa." As I landed the Nitzer inside of the forest outside my father's kingdom walls, my eyes visualized the same sentiments as Gina. As I looked at the different origins of my land I also observed Queen Patano, Lilar, Kilen, Teteman, Fullupian, and Ballajamen land in the other Nitzers. The village people surrounded the Nitzers singing praises. I noticed Gina tries to comprehend the language. At this moment, I was happy she couldn't. Even though the melodies were beautiful to the ear, but the words "My King, you breathe, you're here to rule our lands. To protect us, we are here to serve and love you for eternity." We all exit the Nitzer; the people greeted us coming from every direction of the trees. Singing and dancing. The village was still beautiful as ever. My father's kingdom were filled with all species; Skins, Phantoms, Sand demons and She-ads whom believed in my father's cause and strayed away from negative influences of others. There in the village is also Foldinam four-legged and four-armed creature, Toldinom two-armed and three-legged beasts, Diminutive small creatures and medium with different features. There are also Gliden Phantoms, Phantoms mixed with sand creatures, Mountain-skins resemblance of stone, Firaus stone creatures that's surrounded by fire, and Bar Roots humped over sand creatures.

They came from all over. The skies were bright purplish orange, not what you expect to see on earth. By the filled forests you could tell my father bestowed a definite democracy with different species. The She-ads that believed in my father laws stand guard protecting the walls of Sawdawa. I couldn't believe the village wasn't overtaken by the greed of different species. The trees were of different colors and types; Gray Burgraloots, Maganies blooms, and Yello Zefinallies. As Gina stepped out flabbergasted of what she was seeing, I noticed the pavement was porcelain red. There were flowers of different arrangements, especially my favorite's Liligags, those were of a decent color of peach. Things I hadn't seen in twenty eras. My father's legacy is well respected and kept by Queen Patano, Kilen and his orders, and Dar and his village people. As flower petals rained down upon us, I glanced at Gina's' face and since she's been present in my world she has been handling from the oddities and the creatures we have been coming across on our journey, but for the first time she gives a look of insanity. Her Earth world is extremely unlike our world. She is now observing things she could imagine as fantasy, but now is in the flesh and life.

As the village's people sing praises the kingdom armed guards gather us into a porcelain, gold and diamond chariots, which had silk shades. As Gina, Kilen and I were in; the silk shades were drawn shut. Gina took a breath, she glanced at me, as the chariot moved, and without a second to pass she thought Wow! A King. She looked away, taking in the noise from behind the shade. There was no concentration in her mind at all, she rambled. I could barely read her. She grabbed hold onto a pillow next to her; it was bright red and covered with diamonds and silk. She looked around her she thought loudly that she was out of place. Quickly flowers crept in through the shades, by the hundreds filling the floor and she jumped. The chariot halted with a big thrust after a while. The shades were open, and I stepped out. The village people sang twice as loud as we walked towards the front door of my palace. Rubies, and Onyx stones were tossed on the ground with every step I made, it was what the villagers viewed as welcome gifts, blessings upon returning safe. Confetti drop from the sky, and more praises sang.

    Before I reached the steps it quiet, and I notice everyone fall to their knees. Their head touched the porcelain walk, and they gave thanks in unison as a choir. I see how Queen Patano has been overseeing my fathers' land with the upmost love and ambition to please my father's memories. I heard Gina's thoughts over the rants and raves "it's time to meet his bride. Get prepared." As she speaks it, and as painful it makes me feel to hear her thoughts, it is wise; it will be a good time for her to get prepared. I never had intentions on hurting her. Coming back to my homeland will raise plenty of my deep fears. Not knowing how to be king. Not knowing how to ensure the life of millions. Not knowing how situations with Gina will play out, and not knowing how much Nirew's life has been put on hold for me. I didn't know what to do. Marrying a Being was like blasphemy in my country. The thought of it would cause an outrage. It has always been a historic passing of my world's species, to preserve any parts of our world through time. Beings were considering an invasion of our world. For respect of my origin, Gina was respected. My village people came up to her and shook her hand, and bowed as if she was royalty. Maybe they knew she was the reason I was home. Or maybe it was the fear of upsetting their king. You could tell she was afraid of most that she saw. But I observed her smile and she kept going. I turned to Kilen.

"Kilen will you please show Gina the best room in the palace and make sure she's well-guarded." I said.

"Yes." Kilen said.

As they walked towards the rest quarters in the palace Gina turns observing someone walking towards us as if she was reminiscent of someone she knew. Stepping out of obscurity, "Dar you're alive." I turned to see Dar. "Dar." Gina ran to him and hugged him. She effortlessly touched him. She wasn't afraid of him; in fact, they too had grown close with kinship.

"Hello young one" Dar hugged her back.

"Oh my, I was worried about you." Gina said.

"Destiny has a funny way of giving you added days." Dar said and turns my way "My king, I am happy of your safe arrival."

"Dar I am pleased to see your strong survival." I said.

"Thank you, my king." Dar said, "My king I will help Kilen escort Gina to her quarters in the way to safe guard."

I nod my head at Dar for approval and then they walked; I watched how happy she was to see Dar. I wanted her to have those same feelings for me. I watched her until she was out of my sight. I walked through my home. This was a place I grew from no eras to two-hundred eighty eras. I remembered being in every room of this castle with my father. Where we would meditate, train and talk.

It was so many memories in this palace it hurt to be here, but it was where I belong. I touched the etched out images on the pillars. Every servant bowed in their silk attire as I walked by them. As I turned corners there were countless statues of kings before my father. The detail images on them were remarkable. The way my grandfather sword was drawn in an angle that only Bartarino's knew was a trap to just burst into flames at any time. The left arm raised just right, the right hand holding the sword straight. His father crouched down in a leaping motion with the image of flames shooting from his mouth, his eyes emerald colored and then there was my father. King Ndea Bartarino, standing in a Godly position looking down at an enemy, whom begged for their life. The color of my father's eyes was red, his armor was thick and gold. The spikes on it made with rubies. That image terrified me when I was young.

I continued to walk toward the room where my father slept. I encountered the statue I use to sleep in front of, the image of my mother, Queen Filipara Masa Bartarino. Her skin was fair, and long flowing white hair. It was so life like. She wore a white cloak symbolizing her loyalty to the Phantom family, but it was one thing that stood out about this statue. I stopped walking and stood staring. She held a baby with black hair red eyes, whom smiled at her. She looked reminiscently at the child. He bore silk clothing with a porcelain crown upon his head. That baby was me. I kept on walking to my father quarters when I entered it was still the same. No one had touched it much. The room was semi-preserved from fear of disgracing my father's memory. There were webs, and dust all over certain parts of the portrait of my mother. The servants were careful not to move it out of place. His linen had been preserved as if they had never been moved; the covers were still neatly made exactly the way he would have made it if he were still alive. My mothers' portrait was beside his meditation mat. Where he would meditate in his room. During this time I knew never to enter this room.

As I looked at my mother's picture, I think about all the eras that had passed, never physically knowing if she's still alive. I've heard stories told by villagers and my father's advisors. I've heard my father's cryptic montages of my mother. I only know my deep, bitter, Psychosis thoughts of my mother. I wonder if she's alive. I wonder why my mother left, I wonder out of all the spiritual, magical, supernatural oddities of my world, why isn't anything preserved to give me closing to these thoughts. I have strong feelings of never wanting to see her after leaving me and my father, not after all the love he had for her. I have taken a strong vow to never ever to think of her after my father died. It became more unbearable not to think of her, but it was easier when I left my world. As I look at this picture of my mother it fills me with a vile of what my father would say bubba mister stories. I leaned down and took the picture of her off my father's mat and I threw it and it shattered against the wall. I wanted to burn it with live fire boiling in my veins, but I left his room. I was disappointed that he could love someone so pointless. It reminded me I didn't want to love anyone. I didn't want to go through what my father and I went through over again. I wanted no children, no wife, and definitely no throne. Like a switch it returned me to my original state, I wanted to be alone. Nothing and no one could make me change my mind. I wanted none of that, and I would have stayed in peace and then there was Gina.

****

    We arrived at Aden's home in Sawdawa. It was a castle. There had to be at least 100 rooms, a thousand servants for different things, but no Nirew. I knew everything would change once we arrived here. His future wife, whom he could touch and hold without problems, had more meaning to him. Our kiss was meaningless compared to his promise to his father. I couldn't stand in the way of his father's will for him. Last night Aden and I talked about a lot; he finally opened up a little, about his mom, and his dad. It was more than two sentences this time. I was happy to open up to him and share my feelings about what happened. I had a small closet full of beautiful dresses. At one moment a servant tried to give me a bath and dress me. I had to stop that. I wore the dress that matched Aden's eyes. It was something so appealing. It had a slit in the middle, and it had a full silhouette. I walked around his castle late that night. My hair was still wet from me washing it. I walked the hallways with the water dripping on the floor. The hallways weren't dark, there were little lights lit in the ceiling. I walked to the balcony at the end of the hallway and stood, it overlooked the whole village. The air was nice and clean, and the lights out was so bright, it seem like you were overlooking the strip in Las Vegas.
    "You like it?"
    "It's beautiful" I said.
    "This is a very old country." Queen Patano said.
    "It doesn't look it." I responded.
    "Those garments fit you well."
    "Oh, I didn't notice." But it did.
    "Are you looking for the King?"
    "No, Queen Patano. I'm not looking for Aden. Shouldn't he be with his bride to be?"
    "Lady Nirew is not here." Queen Patano said as she gazed out of the window as she spoke.
    "Oh!" I was surprised.
    "Don't look alarmed. Aden is looking for you now."

"Why, is he okay?" I asked.

"He is fine. You both will be." Aden appeared.

"Hey." He said "Queen Patano." He nodded respectfully.

"Hi." I said.

"Aden." Queen Patano said starring out of the window.

"I see the attire fit you well."

"Yeah, thanks."

"I want to see you privately." Aden said politely.

"Sure." I said following behind him. We walked down a dark hallway; all I could hear were the bottom of my shoes hitting the floor.

"Where are we going I can't see, Aden?"

"Shush!" Aden whispered. Suddenly it became cold, and quiet;

"Aden." Two balls lit up with fire, and then a whole path way. I saw just a small smile from Aden.

"Look around you." Aden said.

"What?" The walls weren't porcelain, they were gray. There was a bed, a fire place, and as I looked around I noticed I was in the room where it all began. It was where Aden had saved me from those two guys that attacked me. The room I was looking for. The room I thought I was imagining. "I was always..."

"In Sawdawa. Yes!" Aden said.

"So why did we have to go through everything we went through?" I asked.

"I couldn't go through the room and risk putting this country in danger."

"How were we here?"

"My father left something. A cube shaped object. It was something his father gave to him. He left it with a man named Suecko I met on Earth. Attached to the cube was a letter and it said "Home would always be with me." I had to heat the cube and think of a safe place and drop the cube. When I did, this room evolved. I don't know how, but it did. I walked out of all the exits and they went everywhere. One door, it was here. The next door, earth and the next door this room and the building." He looked at me for a response.

"Why are you showing me this now?"

"You say I don't open up enough. This was my way of staying apart of my world and running away from it as well." He stopped. "I would sneak around at night just to be in my own space, and when it became too much, I would leave and hunt She-ads."

"What was too much?" I asked watching Aden touch portraits I didn't understand before. They were pictures of his father.

"Being in Sawdawa and living in the same place that my father would never be a part of anymore. I struggled with these thoughts." Aden said balling his fist walking around.

"But some part of you wanted to come home. This room reflects that." I said moving a step closer to him.

"No. It was you having the courage to come to a place you've never been to save your friend. No matter your obstacles, you keep fighting to get her back. Some part of me wants to try to have that courage to be here for my people." He looked at the ceiling. "I talk more now than I ever did. Thanks to the one hundred questions you asked," He smiled "And for you being around."

"You're welcome, I guess." I said.

"Now that is not a compliment. It's more of a cynical remark." He stared at me with a smirk on his face.

"Well I think it is." I smiled.

"You seem to fight your emotions right now, why?" Aden said

"I'm not. It's late. I should go."

"You choose now to withdraw from your feelings."

"It's better this way." I said

"And, may I ask why?"

"We have two separate missions. Mine is to get my friend and leave. Yours is to become what you were destined to be… king." I walked away without looking back at him. I couldn't let him get me thrown off of my goals, and his goals. We were not the reasons of coming to Sawdawa and we couldn't be now.

"You have no objections to these missions?" he asked before I exited the room.

"I'm trying hard not to." I looked at him.

"What if I so choose to have many objections?" He stepped towards me.

"It wouldn't matter. You have promises you must keep. That's clear to me. Good night." I walked down the dim lit pathway. I knew Aden was trying to open up when he showed me that room. I shouldn't love a man that's to be married. I won't be his reason his world wouldn't be stable. He has already given way too much. I'm trying to fight my feelings for him, and as impossible it is to do, I can do it by focusing on what we came here for. I made it back to my room. As soon as I approached my room, Dar stood posted at the door.

"Excellent sunset Gina." Dar said.

"It's been weird, but I guess okay." I said, "And why do you guys call it sunset?"

"You will find in our world we are more with nature than your world. We observe the sun admiration to our lives so what you call nighttime or evening we call sunset. For it's our moment of respect to the Suns rest. For the subject of me being here I have strong admiration for your heart. You have endured and spontaneously witness indescribable events with your eyes that will drive most people to insanity. You have a heart and even still I detect a bit of sadness in you. What is on your mind Being?" Dar asked

"The brave heart you're talking about has always giving me a lonely life. I miss home, I miss the regular feeble things, and most of all I miss Maggie. I, sometimes... I wish I stayed away from Aden like Maggie told me." I shifted on my feet a minute to get comfortable standing in the new flats I was wearing. I was avoiding eye contact with Dar, but then I gathered myself to look at him again, "Maybe, Aden and I wouldn't be so mixed up, and maybe Aden would be on the path that his father dreamed for him and that's Nirew." Dar opened the room doors as I walked in.

"King Aden has always tried to refrain from the journey his father has placed upon him. It's not just your presence that makes him so conflicted with being home. He knows the strength and unity of the species on this planet revolves around his marriage to Nirew even if he doesn't love her. She was born to be part of the Bartarino's. The union of the two will be a legacy kept alive, by our Kings father. It's like, King Ndea's last words. Our people are invested in this fantasy. Now you have been placed in his life, by fate, or Destiny I should say, to shake his world up." Dar laughed.

"What's so funny?"

"You two are holding on to the verity that he made a promise. Being, you two have a lot to endure of the choice in evolution of our world. How many eras are you?"

"I don't know if you know the details of my world I'm from, but I don't date further than President Regan era." I asked, looking at him curiously.

"It isn't more complicated to eras than numbers of years." Dar said, "We symbolize our days and years by staying conscious of our worlds live events…so, we speak in eras instead of years." He added.

"Well, in that case I'm twenty-two." I said.

"Have you ever made a promise, which you had to keep for the sake of others? Promises you knew you wouldn't break because harm may come to someone you love dearly?"

"Yes, I have." I responded.

"This is what Aden has to perceive on his own. Rather to break his promise or keep the heart of his world because it's his own will." Dar said. A knock came from the outer layer of the door, and we glanced over and it was Lilar.

"Dar you are needed by the king." Lilar said.

"Pleasant converse. Good Sunset Gina." Dar said bowing.

"I'm not royalty you don't have to bow."

"Our King has bestowed a grace upon you, you are a Queen. He is the King of our domain, and you will find that our world will respond to you as a Queen." Dar exited the room closing the door lightly behind him.

As hours passed, I lay through the night; the room was warm and dark. I tossed and turned trying to sleep, but the room became warmer, and warmer. Then I saw a shadow sitting right beside my bed. I closed my eyes hoping that it would disappear and prayed that it was just me seeing things. The eyes appeared bright red, and then the dark cloak was visible. "Aden?" I asked.

"Yes, it's me." He said.

"Why do you scare me like that? I thought I was going to die." I sat up in the bed.

"Well, we've been through this conversation before, haven't we?" Aden said sarcastically. "What are you doing in here?" I turn the lantern on.

"You are a guess in our world. I wanted to keep a close eye on how you were adjusting." Aden avoided my glance. I looked at my wardrobe. It was in the same style of clothing he always wore, but it was more presidential and elegant.

"And you couldn't use the door?"

"I prefer my way if you don't mind it?"

"What's with the get up?"

"Before the moments I perceive come to turns." Aden handed me a cloak.

"What is this for? Are you kicking me out?" I smiled.

"No. Just know that no matter what your emotion become for me, or what you perceive of our journey, this is not a gift. It will come a time you will need it." I didn't respond he just seemed very serious when he said it. His eyes brighten for a split second. He long to say something, his stare said so, but he stood up calmly and walked towards the door and vanished. I held the cloak in my hand, and it shocked me, but it was warm, like Aden's presents and his hidden smile. I pulled it closed, and I was wishing it was him. I imagine the kiss we shared, and how I felt with him embracing me the way he did. It was like no other connection I ever had in my life. It felt like love. He wanted to fight it, but a huge part of him loved it and small pieces of ourselves knew that we loved each other, it was apparent.

Chapter 10: Hunt for the Cure

Daybreak came and we all gather in the common room. It was time to strategize on our next mission, which was getting the flower cup from the stream they were growing aside. This operation I needed a few guards there were no room for errors. We were going to a place where deadly animals lived. One thing Earth and Nexima had in common were the wild the animals. We have Jals- big four legged animals, with heads the size of a 1500 pound iron ball. If they stand on their two legs they are at least eight feet, with four fingers with claws that are sharp and deadly. Their teeth are chipped and long. They are very aggressive beasts. The most stubborn animals are the Nosmes and Westtels. Although perception of these creatures from a distance is misleading, they are not small creatures. Their bodies are wide and heavy. Always willing to attack no matter the circumstances. The Nosmes are big headed, three legged animals. It stands on its two back legs and attacks you with the front clawed paw. The pressure from one hit could break all bones. The Westtels are very different and unique animals. It has no legs or claws, it fly's. It attacks with its massive mouth and small teeth, teeth that could chew through metal. Its eyes are big and green, and it's mane is white.

As Dar, Kilen, Teteman, Ballajamen and I attached our weapons to our bodies. I could hear Gina thoughts clearly. She prayed we would all return safely. She didn't want to look at us, in fear of never seeing us again. Quick images of Maggie flew through her head and she tried clearing them fast. She didn't like goodbyes and surely didn't want lasting images of what we were doing now stuck in her head. She kept her eyes closed visualizing positive things, a cross, a Bible, it seems scriptures of protection. It was all so distracting listening and seeing, I didn't hear Dar speaking.

"My King…. My King!" Dar said

"Yes, Dar." I responded

"My King the flower cups are sprouting at midday, they are the best around this time." Dar said.

"Yes, that way they will last long enough to get them back." Lilar said. "Don't forget the flower cup is not to be confused with the

Sesselless. Sesselless has four stems and a gray sprout. The flowercup has six stems attached to it, each stem has a flowercup growing from it and it is blue. Be careful they protect themselves by pointing their nailsheild."

"Dar, Kilen, Teteman, Ballajamen and I will go get the flower, and we will be back. Queen Patano, Gina will stay with you, accompanied by your guardsmen." I said watching Gina sit in the far off corner.

"Of course, if you set off now, you will make it before the animals make it to the stream for their next thirst." Queen Patano said.

We headed out of the doors. I had left Gina in peace with her thoughts. I knew better to spare her the words that we would be fine. I detest that she worried and cared so much about me because time could tell that I would really shattered her heart and thoughts of us. The way she was anxious whenever I'm around and the way she avoided my glances. Whenever I'm standing near, her heart beats faster than I could ever image a heart could beat. The way she tried to clear her thoughts around me.

There was a breeze that shot pass me that cause me to glance back; it was like a natural reaction to this smell now, I seen Gina watching. She stepped away from her place out of sight. She was not the only growing attached... I was too. I see how affectionate Queen Patano and Dar were growing towards her. Kilen kept his distance only because he knew it angered me every time Dar would converse with Queen Patano about her. Kilen did not want to anger me out of respect, but he too was fond of her from afar.

We moved through the Gorge Garden which is about ten miles from the castle which will bring us to the stream. This stream stretched for many distances. This garden was dark and full of thick white clouds that you could barely see through. You could hear the crackling from our feet stepping on branches and walking through the grass. If we pinned pointed our directions right we would end up right in the middle of the stream where the flower cups would sit. They grow on top of each other on both sides; it looks like vines of a big bridge. If you weren't careful how you pick the flower they all would fall apart, die, and you would have to wait four days for them to sprout again. The scent of the flowers brings the animals to the stream where they quench their thirst and eat the flower cups. They usually stay on the opposite ends of the stream, but if they notice anyone around they would cross the stream and attack. This is where the journey gets tough. We had to get there, and get away before the animals reached the stream.

"How long do we have before midday?" I asked.

"Fifteen or Twenty moments at the most." Teteman responded.

"Kilen push ahead. Dar get to my right. Teteman fall back. Ballajamen get to my left. Hold your positions until I say otherwise." I said as we walked through the garden. Kilen was the wisest elder of the Phantoms. As a matter of fact he was the only full blooded Phantom left. He was tall and his white cloak always covered his whole body, leaving nothing visual but his pale wrinkled face and black eyes. He was a silent assassin. He could take out a whole army in his younger eras. That's just how powerful he is. I trust my life with him.

"Animal tracks, sire." Ballajamen said bending down rubbing the soil.

"They have crossed over?" Kilen asked.

"Are they fresh?" I asked.

"Yes. Five moments fresh." Ballajamen said.

"Everyone keep your eyes open?" I said continuing to walk cautiously.

We walked through the garden pushing pass bushel of flowers, listening and watching for wild animals. We still couldn't see much through the fog, but I could smell everything the flowers, the insects, and the water. I observed Dar's glances at me. He longed to ask many questions regarding Gina. Ones to which he knew I would not discuss with him. He knows I can hear them, and he was very curious to what I would say. He finally turned away from me because he knew the consequences of his curiosity.

He thought she would be better suited to leave here, only to spare the Beings heart. Images of Dar standing outside Gina's door and the sounds of her crying filled his visions with hurt on his face for he didn't know what to do. All these images he passed.

"Focus Dar!" I snapped and everyone glanced at us with curiosity.

"My apologies my King." Dar said, he returned his attention to the mission at hand. We were almost to the flower cups.

We heard footsteps in the bushels. We all stopped. Kilen flew through the bushels. Seconds later there was a squeal, and a snap. Kilen appeared with the head of a Nosmes, one of the most hunted creatures for consumption. Its big head and large body can strike once and kill. It's hunted by Stoits which are compared to the Being world's horses and lions. We continued onwards. It was so quiet. A little too quiet for me. Kilen stopped in front of me. Dar looked at him as if he knew what he were feeling.

Dar turned his back towards me, backing close. The others soon followed then, I heard it. There were scurrying footsteps and heavy breathing. The fog blurred my vision. I smelled the flesh of the Spolra-demons. They circled around us. What were they doing in the Gorge Garden? They were forbidden here in the kingdom of Sawdawa. Silence rang out once again, and it was ire, the fog cleared and there all around us, demons. They growled and hissed. Their bodies brawny with claws extended.

"You may not come and squander amongst these lands." Kilen spoke.

"I, Doblar-me have come to seek the revenge for the death of my brothers." He said as he stepped forward. "Now, which of you executioners; will accept the price you so desperately set upon your own brow?"

"Your brother's withheld the king himself from returning to claim his right to the throne." Ballajamen spoke.

"The king... There is no King of Sawdawa. There is only a desolate memory of the one who held the throne." Doblar-me said and I got angry. "This adolescent, this child.... This... would be king. He would never rule if he wanted to. Not as long as we are alive."

"Enough. I have no coil with you and your kingdom. Leave my realm or you shall have grave consequences." I said. Doblar-me looked to his right and nodded, one of his brothers stood in front of him. He stretched his arms and extended his claws. Kilen stepped forward. Doblar-me brother stretched his arm towards Kilen and he moved quickly. A second later the brother was on the ground. Kilen had used a ritual to double his form and he snapped the brother's neck and returned to where he was standing. We were close by the flowercups, you could smell them.

Another one of the Spolra-demons attacked and Dar grabbed him by the neck with his top hands, lifted him with the bottom arms and ripped his arms from his body and tossed him next to his dead brother. Ballajamen turned toward the demon in front of him, eager to be the next to attack. He turned to look at me, his eyes full with a white glow. He was ready to use his ability to shock the body with one glance. "No." I said. "This is not over. We will have revenge. And no one will be with you when we do, prince Aden." Doblar-me said. They all moved back into the fog. And you heard their footsteps scurry away. Their brothers laid bloody on the grounds. I hoped it wasn't enough blood to bring the animals out.

We walked and once we reached the flower cups, I snapped three cups precisely from the end of the root. I placed it in a slender glass with water, and cap it so it would be safe on our journey back.

We headed back. "That was a little too simple." Kilen said.

"Yes, perhaps you're right to say that." I responded looking around.

"Everything doesn't have to be so hard young Aden." Dar said, even though I knew the real reason behind what he said. Kilen squealed and circled around us sweeping dust around. The noise he made was deafening to the ears. He yelled take cover and brought up more dust shielding us.

"What's wrong Kilen?" I asked.

"Aden, Falsla. They smell the flower cups." Teteman yelled jumping beyond the dust. A Falsla made it through the dust running for the flower cups. Falsla were long four legged, hairy beasts whose shoulders are broad and metal like to the touch. Their drool was like acid. Just the touch of it burned. Their eyes are slanted and orange. "Dar take the flowers now, get it to the castle." I said tossing the glass to him.

"I won't leave you my king." Dar yelled.

"That's an order." I yelled over the noise.

Ballajamen took on the first Falsla, by the time the dust settled there were two more approaching. One flew and clawed my chest, and the other attacked my back. I was bitten a few times as I fought back. We all were fighting them off as Dar proceeded to get the flower cups to the castle. He ran up the hills. Kilen fought two. Teteman had been torn limb from limb by three Falslas that had snuck up and attacked him. They had flown around him in a circle snacking on him as if he were the flowers. A Westtels had roared from behind us, but had not crossed the stream. Westtels were pups of the Falslas beasts.

"My King, get out of here." Kilen said

I watched how all of the animals were gathering. I was being pent down. I was grazed. I knew that if I didn't do something we would be killed, but what could I do? We were outnumbered. We had come too far. Kilen used his strength to break necks. He used his sword to slash them one by one. The image of Gina ran across my face. I grew angry, my hands lit, then pain surged through my face, then my body grew, and exploded with fire.

****

The floor shook, and the castle vibrated and suddenly everything stopped. I wondered if they had earth quakes. No one appeared to be too bothered by the rumbling; I stood at the window staring in the distance. I wondered if Maggie was holding on. I was wondering if she had already died. It had been over a week here since we've been on our journey. It's been two days since on Earth. Maggie's doctors didn't have a chance to see she was sick. She was taking for ransom. The She-ads king Poncho-.. Whatever his name. He wants Aden. I wondered if she had awakened and had been alright. I don't think they would kill her until Aden showed his face. My mind was racing until I saw smoke in the distance. "Wow, what is that smoke over there?" I asked pointed from the tower.

"I have no idea." Lilar said. "It seems to be a great deal of smoke. What do you think of it my Queen?"

"It's the great mountain fires. They smoke every few days. Gina as volcanoes does on Earth. Our mountains smoke." Queen Patano said. The smoke still seemed out of the ordinary. I've never heard of smoking mountains, Nexima differs greatly from Earth. I hear everyone say they are similar, but I don't see it. The doors burst open from the front. I couldn't hear what was going on, so I ran towards them. There were yelling and panic.

"What's going on?" I asked looking at Queen Patano.

"Worry not Gina, just go to your quarters." Queen Patano said.

"Dar, where's Aden?" I stood, my heart raced from not seeing his face. No one said anything.

"Where's everyone?"

"We were attacked, and I have to get back." Dar said handing over a vase and running out.

"Aden!" I said running towards the door.

"Dekcol moor." Lilar said, stretching his arms towards me.

I stood isolated in a room. One minute I'm at the front doors, and the next I'm in a concrete room. I ran looking for the doors, but there were none. I yelled, but no one ran to my aid. He locked me in this room. I sat against the concrete wall. All I could imagine was never seeing Aden again. If he died, I'm the one to blame. "Let me out, now." I cried slapping the palms of my hands on the walls, still no one responded. It seemed I had been yelling and crying forever, I settled against the wall, and didn't move. The crying and yelling tired me, and I lay silently on the floor. I tried fighting sleep but I couldn't, I drifted. I was walking in a place full of beautiful flowers, of different colors. I smiled looking at the white gown I wore as I strolled down the path that appeared as I walked. There was a mirror on one side I noticed that my hair was straight with a porcelain tiara on it. Aden stood at the end of the pathway in a white shirt that was half button, and white pants, his hair was a reddish/black color. His features were beautiful. He was younger looking than I had ever seen. He reached for my hand. His chest had marks on it. They looked like stabbed wounds. His eyes were dark red, not at all the colored they use to be, and he whistled a tune as I walked up to him. He had a circlet on his head. He grabbed my hand, twirled me in a full circle. Our eyes met. He had kissed me.

"You... you touched me." I said amazed.

"I will always be able to touch you. Because I love you." He said.

"I don't understand. What about Nirew. What about the rules of your world?"

"Don't question everything. Just let us be." He smiled.

"I'm sorry. I always do that don't I?" I smiled.

"I have to go, tell me you love me, because we may never see each other again." His eyes became watery.

"No, we will see each other, don't say that." I cried as he faded away.

"Tell me Gina." He yelled.

"I do, I do love you." I yelled to him, but he had already faded away. I had awakened; I was unaware of where I was at first. I remembered being in a concrete room, with no doors, yelling and banging on them. Now I was in my room. I ran towards the door and grabbed the handle, but it wouldn't open. I sat on the other side of the door and just watched it. "Aden come home safe. I will never forgive myself if you died. Please come home. I care for you."

****

I heard Gina voice. I lay on the ground. "Gina!" I looked around. "Please come home." "Gina."

I yelled. I saw a Falsla in pieces on top of me. I pushed it off of me, and rolled off of one that lay underneath me. I stood up, and I was in a crater. I stumbled all over the place. "Kilen! Ballajamen!" I yelled falling on the ground, trying to focus my eyes.

"My king." Dar ran towards me. The ground shook. Dar stood still for a minute looking around him.

"What happen?"

"My king." Kilen appeared.

"I'm well..." Ballajmen said, "Teteman didn't make it."

"You are bleeding let's get you back to the castle." Dar said lifting me. I yelled with the pressure of his grasp around my body.

We entered the castle a little while later, and I been placed upon a table. Lilar started looking at my wounds. He looked at Queen Patano and said, "He cannot repair himself. It has finally come to be." Everyone shook their heads.

"What are you talking about?" I manage to get the words out of my mouth.

"Lilar, stitch him, before his wounds spoil." Queen Patano said.

"Aden!" Gina yelled running towards me. She was crying.

"Get her out of here." I yelled as Lilar cleaned my wounds. I tried not to scream from the pain in front of her.

"No, don't touch me. Aden let me stay. Please." She cried.

"Get her out now." The pain shot through me.

"No!" She cried.

"I'm sorry; you need not to see him like this." Dar said grabbing her and removed her from the room. I saw the tears in her eyes as she struggled to get away from Dar. She left kicking and screaming.

"Give me something for the pain." I said. Lilar said a ritual for healing medicine that put me to sleep. I dreamt of nothing. When I opened my eyes Gina was sleeping in a chair next to my bed. I knew the way she was curled up in the chair she was cold. Her hair fell in her face. She was dressed in a blue silk gown. She must have been there all night. When I sat up the bed squeaked and she jumped up.

"Aden." She said.

"Hey." I said.

"How are you feeling?" She had a look of concern.

"I'm better. Have you been here all sunset?" I asked her.

"Yes. I was worried." She looked at the wounds on my body as I held my shoulder that throbbed with pain.

"I'm okay."

"I wish I could hug you right now." She said walking towards the window.

"Gina." I followed her wishing she didn't feel that way, but I did as well; it was an initial reaction lately, to her kind words and affection for me.

"Don't Gina me. I was so worried about you. You should've let me stay at your side." She rolled her eyes at me.

"You shouldn't had been in there. I don't want you to concern yourself so deeply with me." I responded to her.

"You should've let me stayed. Stop pushing me away."

"Gina!"

"Stop saying my name like that. When Dar came back alone, I was terrified and he Lilar me in a room because I was trying to come after you."

"I'm happy they stopped you or you would have been killed." I snapped at her insistence.

"Whatever." She turned away from me.

"You must understand sometimes you can get yourself in treacherous situation." My patience grew short.

"There's a reason for everything Aden." She snapped, then quickly calmed herself, "Look, I can't... I can't help it when it comes to you." She starred away from me.

"Why don't you go get rest Gina? Worry yourself no more of my well-being." I said watching her gasp a little looking at me and she walked away. She stopped at the door.

"I'm happy, you're okay." Gina left the room. I had a lot of questions to ask. I approached Lilar and Queen Patano.

"What happen yesterday?" I asked.

"When?" Lilar asked.

"I woke up in a hole. You said it has finally happened. What happened?"

"You never were able to adapt to the Fira side of your family. Now you have finally absorbed additional powers." Queen Patano said.

"What other powers are there?" I asked.

"We are unsure. You are almost ready to face Ponchopalapare. There is just a little left you need to have. It will all be added unto you soon." Queen Patano said.

"What are you talking about?" I asked.

"You have unlocked your father's ability to burst into flames." Dar said.

"I don't even know how I did it. Why didn't someone tell me that?" I asked.

"We were told that three great things would happen to you. What things, we aren't certain." Queen Patano said.

"Maggie's days are growing short." Lilar said, "I'm making the medicine now. It will take at least three more days."

"I have three more days until dooms day." I walked away, everything was about to change. I could feel it.

****

I tried to figure out how did someone I thought was so incredibly strong, get hurt the way Aden did. I couldn't understand it. It was all puzzling. I stood out on the balcony for fresh air. I was so distracted I didn't hear Aden approach. I stood there for a while, and so did he. He stood in silence. "A penny for your thoughts." He said.

"What?"

"Oh, that's a saying on earth. When you want to know what has their thoughts occupied?" He smiled.

"Oh." I looked at him; he stood out in white. His hair was straight, and he was just tall and handsome. His shirt was halfway button; you could see the thickness of his chest. There was a scar in the middle. I stared, and he turned away remembering my dream.

"It doesn't hurt as bad." He said.

"Oh, that's good." I looked away.

"You worry too much." He focused his eyes straight on me.

"I know that's a bad quality, isn't it." I laughed.

"It could be."

"You're too carefree." I said.

"That's so I don't worry myself to death."

"Well I worry so I'm not too carefree."

"Why walk around worrying if you're doing something, you may cause a certain reaction?" Aden asked.

"Because if you don't you could hurt someone, or get someone poisoned like I did." I said starring at Aden, and he snapped his head towards me.

"Will you lay off that, please?"

"Well, it is my fault, isn't that what you said? He turned his head away from me.

"Let's not rehash the past. Let's take a walk." he said changing the subject.

"That sounds like a good thing." I said exhaling, and taking one last look outside. I was happy to change the subject. We walked to an exit on the far side of his castle. It was a room painted white with nothing in it. The walls were bare. I looked around, and he smiled.

"Do you like flowers?" Aden asked and flowers appeared as he walked around the room.

"How about a little sun?" The sun shined through the glass window on the ceiling.

"Aden, this is wonderful... Aden!" I said looking around for him, "Aden, how did you do that?"

"Come here, let me show you something." I watched him as I strolled down the pathway looking around. Everything resembled the things in his world. The pathway I walked down look like gold porcelain with a shiny look on top of it. The flowers I smelled walking towards him were mahogany and like a breath of fresh air. It was just like the dream I had. When I approached him, he pointed to the ceiling. "Look there."

"It's dark… Its Nexima stars. Its daylight out, how are there stars in here?" I asked looking at him.

"It's unexplained. You believe in the unexplained don't you?" He asked me.

"Yes. Because… of you, I do." I looked at him, and he avoided my glare.

"All you have to do is channel your emotions to how you're feeling right now." Aden said walking around.

"What do you mean?" I asked

"Close your eyes and focus on something, anything." Aden spoke I closed my eyes and I found an image I could focus on, it was Maggie and I having a fight over the obsession with the abandon building, but even through that. I found someone I cared about and Aden's face appeared. I pictured him and Maggie meeting and being friends. I thought of him and I, what I wish it could be like. In an instance, I remembered being locked in a room, pounding on the walls, praying to see Aden again. My eyes shot opened, and I saw cloudy skies, with a drizzle of rain.

"Is this my emotions?" I asked.

"You shouldn't feel that way. I'm fine." Aden said.

"I was locked in a room, terrified about you." I walked towards him.

"Lilar did what he needed to, to keep you safe." He walked behind trees that appeared when he moved.

"Yeah, I'm still kind of angry about that."

"It was for good reasons, so you can't be too angry." He said watching my every move.

"How long has it been since I've been here?" I asked.

"About two weeks."

"Is that how long it has been on earth too?"

"No, on earth it's about three days." He smirked.

"What's so funny?" I asked.

"Your curiosity amazes me. Even though, you still don't quite understand my world yet."

"If you would talk more, maybe I would."

"I have my priorities in place." Aden said.

"I like to see you smile, instead of being so serious." I said, changing the subject. I knew his priorities didn't mean me.

"You want to know something I like about you?" He walked towards me handing me a flower.

"What?" I placed the flower in my hair as we stood face to face.

"You're brave."

"You think so?" I said staring at him as he looked at me so intensely.

"But, your bravery can cause you great harm."

"Why are you so scared to admit how you feel about me?" I asked.

"I'm not frightened at all. I choose to keep down confliction in your life." He said as I looked around as the scenery in the room changed. It changed from a park like area, to a room, and to a waterfall. We stood in a pool of water.

"What confliction? What would I be conflicted about?"

"More questions. You always will have more." He stood face to face with me and smirked. He always avoided my questions with snide remarks.

"What's going on in here?" I said pointing to the waterfall.

"The room is trying to adjust to our emotions." He said.

I tried not to get excited about Aden being so close, but I couldn't help myself. The water had risen to my ankles as the waterfall fell behind Aden. I loved looking into his eyes; it was a story behind them; with the color, the shape of his eyelids, and his skin tone. I knew he could hear my heartbeat every time he was near me. He was so close, but yet so far. I could never get him to admit any feeling for me. I felt like a girl with this huge crush on one of the football players in school that would never look my way. If only I could get him to say something that I could remember after I left here. Something could tell me I wasn't crazy for feeling the way I did for him. The water level had risen to my knees. It was nice and warm, I bet because he was next to me. The room changed from the sun setting, to a waterfall under the moon, and stars. Aden stood in front of me because he read my mind. He wanted to say something.

"Your thoughts can be very bothersome, but I am compassionate towards that... Look at that?" He paused "The moon, stars, and water. This is your emotion right now."

"How can you figure?"

"You like a relaxing setting."

"What do you like?" I asked, as soon as I asked candles floated in midair.

"You are feeling this. Very ….uh, in your world they would say…. romantic." Aden's was intense, but perfect for this moment.

"Do you know what romance is?"

"I know. Our worlds aren't that different." He laughed.

"Oh!" I smiled looking down in embarrassment.

"Even though I was a jerk to you, you still stuck around. Why?"

"You seem like you needed a friend. I don't know, maybe because I'm weird." I said.

"You're far more than peculiar… There's a reason for everything, I can't figure out the reasons for our encounter yet." Aden eyes sparkled; he looked as if he was trying hard to focus. More like trying to read me. In a perfect world we would kiss and make this uncomfortable moment cozier. He knew what I wanted, and I didn't care if it hurt. I would risk it to have him touch me again. He laughed. Aden was giving into my thoughts as he moved his lips closer to mine. "Tell me too." He placed one hand on the tree behind my head, and one on the tree behind my waist. I felt the warmth of his body heat covering mine as he moved closer.

"Are you happy about us encountering each other?" I asked as his hand reached for my neck, I felt the steam. He closed his eyes and he moved in to close the deal, but the doors burst opened. "Lady Nirew awaits you my king in your chamber." A servant said. He opened his eyes and I looked at him. He turned away and looked down, trying to avoid my stare. "Go to her!" I whispered trying not to cry because we were interrupted before he could answer my question or even kiss me, but it was that time I knew would come.

"I'll be there, thank you." Aden backed away from me.

"We forgot about her that quickly." I said, the water had disappeared, but my dress was still wet. Aden said nothing, he walked away. We seemed to let the main factor fade away, but now it was a huge part of our division. I couldn't like him, or even love him ever again, and all he could do was lust from far away. His servant was the beginning of our separation.

Chapter 11: Lady Nirew

I entered my quarters and Lady Nirew stood awaiting my arrival. She was my height, with long silky hair, braided into a ponytail with a ribbon at the end. Her eyes were brown, and her body was slender, shapely and her skin was bright yellow. It seemed a sin to have such a beautiful mate. As I approached her, she bowed. She was so happy to see me. Lady Nirew jumped up and hugged me. It was something I did miss. She was the only girl I've ever known who could. I was excited to see her, because she and I had been apart for many eras, but still she waited for me. With no communication at all, I kept myself away from her for eras, but she's still here for me.

"My King, oh I've missed you so much." Lady Nirew said jumping up and down. "Why are you so wet?"

"I've missed you too Lady Nirew." I smiled avoiding the last part of her question.

"Oh, I cannot wait to marry you, and start our lives together, my king." She said.

"It will be soon Lady Nirew. We have much to discuss." I said.

"We do, I must tell you all the things that's been happening since you've been away." Lady Nirew grabbed my hand and we sat down. It was weird that most from my world could touch me, and certain creatures couldn't. I still couldn't wrap that reality around my head. It has something to do with the curse that had been placed upon me. No one knows how to undo what was done, only my father.

"Okay and I must discuss some things with you."

"Oh, I have missed you." she kissed me and we shared that kiss for moments, until my thought traveled upon Gina and her feelings for me.

"What is wrong my king, you don't gesture back." She said, I hadn't noticed I pulled away from her.

"Lady Nirew, I have a guest in my home, and she's…"

"She?" Lady Nirew backed away and searched my eyes.

"Yes, she… She is a Being." I said.

"A Being, Is it on a leash? Have you brought me a new pet?" She smiled.

"No, she is not a pet! She is not on a leash, and I want you to treat her with respect."

"Surely my king, you cannot be serious..." she gave a short laugh "And what am I to tell my acquaintances when they arrive to see you home? That we have a guest… that you have broken one of the most forbidden laws that this world has stood on for generations?" she snapped. "I sincerely won't be bothered with what you tell your acquaintances. She is my guest and you, along with everyone else will respect her as long as I am King. She has heart, and soul, but among everything, she is feisty and won't be afraid to speak her mind to anyone. She is from Earth." I walked away from the chair.

"You speak as if you have befriended this thing." Lady Nirew followed behind me.

"Her friend has been captured by the She-ads because of me. I have grown fond of her because she has been kind, even when I pushed her away and was an insolent prick." I looked to Lady Nirew.

"She was kind to me in her world, and so shall everyone be in this one to her."

"I want to meet this Being. Does she have a given?" Lady Nirew looked vindictive as she spoke.

"It's Gina." I turned away from her.

"Take me to her Aden." Lady Nirew said firmly.

"Let's go to the common room and show everyone else you're here. You will meet Gina there." I said grabbing her hand. We walked down the hallway and Lady Nirew talked and talked. She spoke of how she was helping her father put together his special plans for us after our wedding. She said it was a surprise.

We entered the common room where Queen Patano, Dar, Kilen and Gina sat. It was silent. Dar and Kilen bowed to her. Gina's face was flushed as she sat next to Dar. She looked at Lady Nirew and turned away. Queen Patano grabbed Gina hand, and gave her a pat of sympathy. Everyone sat quietly, no one made a sound. Dar stared at Gina, but she said nothing. His heart ached for her. He felt she was in pain and only wanted to comfort her. Even Kilen had empathy for the Being.

"Hello everyone, you shouldn't bow, I am not Queen yet." Lady Nirew said, and then she turned her head towards Gina.

"You are the Being Aden has been telling me about." Her tone was rough and annoyed.

"Well, don't just sit there. You are lesser than we, so you must bow before me."

"Lady Nirew." I said looking towards her.

"I don't bow." Gina clenched her jaws.

"My King, are you not going to make her show me respect, or must I tie it to the tree and beat it out of her." Lady Nirew snapped putting her hands on her hips.

"The only way you'll get me to bow to you is if you hop on one leg, and bark like a dog." Gina walked up to her and stared her straight in the eyes.

"You sure are a feisty little insolent thing aren't you?" Lady Nirew moved closer towards Gina, but Gina didn't back down. They were ready to brawl. "I shall befriend you."

"Lady Nirew, Please." I grabbed her. I knew that comment didn't mean kinship at all.

"Aden, you better put that one on a leash. She may try to run away once I'm through with her." Gina said as she glanced at me and back at Lady Nirew and walked away. That was out of character for Gina was never so serious before, not around me. Out of all the things she seen for the first time, and was terrified of, Lady Nirew size and stature didn't make her quench of fear at all.

"Aden dear, you stare like you've seen a wild animal." Lady Nirew said, but I didn't pay her any attention, I stared off into the distance as Gina disappeared.

"Aden!" She snapped her fingers in my face.

"Yes Lady Nirew." I said focusing my attention on her.

"You are discomforting me." She looked unhappy.

"I'm sorry, let's get prepared for your guest." I said.

"That's better." Lady Nirew smiled. "Queen Patano, would you move over, I'm home now. You're not head of the table anymore beloved."

"Lady Nirew! Please." I said.

"What? Is it not my right to sit at the head of the table as my King?"

"Don't worry my King. I will check on Gina." Queen Patano excused herself.

"Queen Patano." I heard her thoughts. She was disappointed in me, but what was I to do?

"Let her chase after the puppy." Lady Nirew sat down. She snapped her fingers to a servant to get his attention. I knew this would be very uncomfortable. "Sit my King." Although I didn't like what had just transpired between the two of them, I knew Nirew did it out of happiness and love of me. I must admit I missed her very much even though a lot has happened over these last weeks. I made a promise I must keep. As I sat the servants placed food before us, and Nirew looked at me as I watched her.

"My king, is there something unfitting to your likes upon your supper?" She asked.

"I am fine Nirew. I can't get over the beauty I see before my eyes." I smiled.

"Stop my king, I might actually believe your kind words."

"These feelings are not meant to be taken lightly." "Trust me my highest, they are not."

"May I excuse myself my king?" Dar said as he too was unhappy. I nodded.

****

Aden couldn't possibly love Nirew. She was rude and arrogant. She wanted me to bow to her. You could tell that she didn't hear about me that she didn't know who I was. But who am I on this planet anyway? I was nobody to anybody. I had to be a lady and walk away. Who knows what kind of power she had, she could probably pummel me to death. I didn't care if I ever saw her on the streets on Earth, she and I would have it out. Aden would never look at me the same if I would handle her like I handled girls on earth. I wanted so bad now to get Maggie and go back home and let Aden and his bride start their life. A knock came to the door. I said nothing. The door opened, and it was Queen Patano. She came in and closed the door and stood with no words to say. I said absolutely nothing either.

"My dear Gina." She spoke.

"No, I don't want to hear it. Don't you dare take up for him." I snapped.

"It is unsettling to see you angry like this. This is temporary. You set that in your mind."

"So what, I'm supposed to walk around and act like this doesn't affect me?"

"I am not asking you to set aside your heart's desire. You must stay focus for Being Maggie." I heard her name, and I slid down to the floor.

"I'm trying to and can't help what I feel." I whispered as my tears fell. "Please just leave."

"He has not made a definite choice… if that may sooth your pain." Queen Patano walked out. I climbed into bed and I went to sleep to clear my thoughts. Help, help me Gina. I jumped up from bed. It sounded a lot like Maggie, but how could I hear her? I ran from my room towards her screaming, and I couldn't find her. I called out to her "Maggie. Maggie where are you." I'm here. I walked into a room, and there Maggie stood. She stood in a hospital gown with her arms stretched out. Gina, I've missed you. When are you going to get me out of here? "Maggie how did you get here? We can leave now. Let me tell Aden, you're here." I'm locked in a glass; I can't get out of here. Gina you have to save me before it's too late. I notice a glass box around her and it was green liquid filling the glass container. She screamed and beat on the glass. "Maggie. " I said running towards her and she disappeared. I screamed looking around for her. "All you have to do is hand Aden over and you can get this thing back." A tall creature stepped from behind the shadows. "What did you do with her?" I asked. You have two days before she's dead. The creature revealed himself and I screamed. He had no eyes, and he stood with great posture, he had to be over ten feet tall. His hands were an odd shape. His skin sagged like burnt meat. He reached for me, and I fell to the ground screaming.

"Gina! Gina!" I had awakened Dar, Queen Patano, and Kilen surrounded me. I hugged Dar.

"Being what frightens you?" Dar asked holding me tightly.

"Maggie! She called out. I couldn't save her. It's my fault." I cried "This thing had her."

"What thing?" Kilen stared.

"He was a huge creature..." I exhaled.

"Oh no!" Queen Patano said.

"What?" Dar looked at her.

"He has gotten through Maggie's mind into Gina's. This is not good." Queen Patano said.

"What's going on?" Aden glided through the door armed with two Emerald blades.

"I want to get Maggie and leave this place." I cried.

"Gina." Aden approached me looking concerned. He was shirtless and all his battle scars showed.

"Let them take care of her Aden." Lady Nirew grabbed his arm. She too was barely clothed. I didn't even want to image what had transpired between them. I looked at Aden as guilt was written on his face, but I turned away because it wasn't important right now.

"Ponchopalapare came to her in a dream…" Queen Patano said.

"What?" Aden Yelled "How?"

"He came through the Beings friend." Kilen said.

"What did he say?" Aden gently tugged away from Lady Nirew.

"My King, let's go back to bed. Let them handle it." Lady Nirew said.

"Gina, what did he say?" Aden stood close. "He wants me to trade you for Maggie and he said we have two days before she dies." I wiped my eyes.

"No!" Lady Nirew said "You will die. I just got you back."

"What is it you think we should do my king?" Kilen asked.

"I promised Gina I would save Maggie…and that's what I will do." Aden didn't look my way; he just walked out of the room.

"I shall return. My Queen, will you please stay with her?" Dar asked.

"Of course, those words need not be spoken." Queen Patano whispered.

Dar and Kilen left the room. It had become freezing and it felt awkward with it being the queen, Lady Nirew and I. Lady Nirew walked back and forth saying nothing. She paced. Queen Patano searched for words to say, you could tell it was written over her face, I never thought I would see the day she would have nothing to say.

"Don't let him do this Being. He is to be wed to me. I have waited eras for him." Lady Nirew begged.

"Lady Nirew!" Queen Patano said.

"I love him, and he would die saving your friend. You will have your friend, and I would have loss my life. What is it you want? I will give you anything." Lady Nirew cried.

"I want nothing, but to leave this place with my friend." I said.

"She may have already perished. Please go home, and let us be." She wiped her tears.

"Can you leave my room please?" I asked. I felt bad because I was in a position of giving and taking a life. I would have never thought God would put me in such an awkward position. Lady Nirew stormed out of the room. I hugged my knees close. I didn't know what to do. Queen Patano still sat by my side and said nothing even though she knew the thoughts going through my head. She wanted me to talk, but I sat silent. The room became colder. This was the first time since I've been here, that this room wasn't warm. It bothered me I would have to lose someone I loved to save someone I love. Aden for this little time had become my highlight for waking each day. He was my strength. He was my hope of getting Maggie back. He was my friend.

"Gina, you mustn't worry. Our king will do what he can." Queen Patano said holding my shoulders.

"What if he dies? I would never forgive myself." I cried.

"King Aden is very skilled. He won't go down without a fight."

"And if he loses this fight…." I asked with tears running from my eyes.

"Then he will be remembered for keeping his promise and being a noble King." Queen Patano looked away.

"Do you think that he can win?" I asked looking at Queen Patano, she sat in silence. "He can't, can he?"

"Do not mistake my silence as your answers. It may lead you astray. King Aden, will be fine." She replied. Her facial expression filled with uncertainty, I knew it and I'm sure she knew I could see it.

Later, I walked to the common room and seen all Sawdawa soldiers standing armed. Aden had been talking a long time. He strategizes on how rescuing Maggie would go, but for the night everyone was to be on the lookout no one was to sleep. The room cleared out and Aden and I are left alone. He barely looked at me, he said nothing. Then he straightened his postured standing tall, he had his hands at his side and he stared at me. His hair was wet, long and curly. His glance was blank, with no love, no life.

"Aden, I don't want you to die." I said, but he laughed "What's so funny?"

"Gina, I don't mean this to be discourteous, but this is not a good time." He turned away.

"Make it the time." I said.

"What do you think, I will rescue your friend and make it out of there alive. It's not the movies you Beings watched. This creature is dangerous." Aden snapped.

"We're back to the Being thing again… What happen to you calling my name?" I walked next to him.

"Gina, I didn't mean it like that." Aden said.

"I want to make some kind of plan so you don't die."

"You and I will never be, so why not get your friend and live happily ever after." He yelled.

"Don't be a jerk. And why can't I have you? Is it because you made a stupid promise? Some promises are meant to be broken. Yeah, news flash Aden! Your father made you make promises, because he knew one day you would break them to live, your life not his." I yelled.

"You didn't know my father, so don't you dare speak of him." He said.

"Have you ever once listened to what your friends told you? Oh no, wait! You're too hot head to listen to anyone."

"Don't lecture me Gina, go away." Aden faced me.

"Listen Aden. You decide for yourself in life, not…"

"Get out!" Aden yelled and the room shook and his eyes lit like fire in a fire place and the lights dimmed and returned to their normal shade. "I want you out of here. Stay absent from my sight. I need time to gather my thoughts." He said with so much anger and force.

"You don't scare me." I said.

"What do I have to do? Set you on fire? Or do you want to be ripped apart? Any one of those I could do to get my point across." His eyes got brighter.

"Listen to me."

"Do you love me?" He asked, but I didn't respond, I was caught off guard. "Do you love me?" he yelled, but I still said nothing "Good, because right now, I don't have a warm spot in my heart for you. Not anymore. I know what my father did. I don't need you to tell me. Do you think I'm naive, like I'm one of the male species on Earth? I'm far more advanced. I'm not playing games with you. My father made me make this promise, not for happiness, but peace for my country, to sit on his throne with power and dignity." He laughed "Look at you, you're so condescending…you can't even admit how you feel about me, but you want to address me, as if I'm a man without a reason. I will save your friend, and then I will send you home, and forget you ever existed." His eyes stayed lit with anger.

"Aden." I whispered and I couldn't believe what he had said. Those words hit me and I was out of breath. Like my chest was caving into my lungs, stopping me from inhaling and exhaling "Fine." Tears ran down my face "I see why you chose Nirew, you're both alike. Bitter old fools. Looks like I got my answer, you weren't happy that we encountered each other, by the lack of your clothing." I walked away, but I turned, "Yes, I loved you. But now, I'm not so sure anymore." He glanced up at me with a face of regret as if he wanted to apologize. I walked away. It was much too late for an apology now.

Chapter 12: Special Guests

Aden was having a huge gathering at his castle today. I tried to stay tucked out of the way after the words that were spoken last night. Decorations were put up everywhere, servants were scurrying around. I sat on the balcony by my room so that as soon as I heard anyone I could sneak back in without troubles. When Aden admitted himself to my face that he had little feelings for me and I immediately replied him the same, deep inside me knew that it was all out of anger. I, however don't know if Aden meant the words he said. It was all so mind boggling, but I had to take it for what it was. I knew that in an instant after the dream encounter with Ponchopalapare Aden was coming to terms with the idea of never breathing again. Let alone keeping his promise to Nirew and his late father. I contemplated about all the things he was giving up... just for me. For Maggie, we, I was beneath his kind. At the moment, I wondered what Aden was feeling, what was going through his mind? He and his fiancé was preparing for her friends.

"Gina, why do you isolate yourself from everyone?" Dar asked as he approached.

"I rather be out of the way don't you think it's best?" I said.

"Why do you feel that its best when you are an honored guests by our king young one?" Dar asked.

"They are Nirew's friends. She doesn't like me, and neither will they."

"Young one, so you don't just stare into the air, why don't we go out unto the village." Dar said.

"I would like that very much. Will it be safe?" I asked.

"You will have me and guardsmen at your every step." Dar replied.

"Ok." I stood from my seat. I walked at Dar's side. As we approached the door, we passed Aden whom sat with Nirew. I glanced at them and she didn't look my way because she was talking, but he gave me a brief look. I turned and decided not to worry anymore.

I walked the village with Dar, he showed me around the squares just to get my mind off of last night. This wasn't your normal village. It's wasn't at all like Berut Mountains. This village looked like New York. There were huge buildings like stores. Only there material was molded from natural life. Rocks merged, Buildings made out of sticks it seemed, but more modern, the windows were like birthstones. It was so beautiful. We went into a lot of the buildings, they were structurally sound. The floors were clean, gorgeous, smooth sand. The walls were porcelain. In these buildings, there were beautiful cloths of clothing being sold, things people would not sale on Earth. These creatures work, not for payment, but to have something to do with their time. Although money was greatly appreciated, they still will give to make sure their people had enough. The flowers were beautiful, and the scent was of bake goods. Dar treated me to varieties of food, and desserts. Some of which looked to disgusting to even try. Every stepped I made the sun shined so brightly. It was beautiful to hear how these creatures congregated amongst each other. Their children played while their parents worked or shopped. This felt like some kind of relation to home. Dar and I laughed and talked, he was my only friend since I've been here.

"How do you feel Gina?" Dar asked.

"I'm very sad here. You are the only one that cares anything about me." I said.

"I doubt very much that is true." He smirked. "Queen Patano admires you and King Aden…"

"Let's not talk about him right now ok?" I whispered.

"I will respect you want that peace right now… but can I also say, I find comfort in you." Dar said.

"Why is that?"

"You remind me a lot of my daughter Kyya."

"Really? How is that?" I asked as we walked along the pathway.

"She was confident, friendly, she and I had a very good relationship and she too was in love… let me tell you a story about her. Kyya's mother couldn't tend to her one day, and she had to be with me while I trained with King Ndea, that's Aden's father. She watched as we fought. When I fell to the floor, I observed her tears falling from her face. She ran to me, and screamed at King Ndea, "Don't hurt my baba." But all the king did was laugh. He pulled her to the side and told her he was teaching her baba how to protect her, and if she wanted his son Aden could teach her. She said she wanted to learn because she wanted to protect me. I refused at once. But she begged. So I let her train. Aden had become her best friend, and he taught her well. She grew to love him, and only found comfort in him. He made her feel important and very secure with herself. Then Lady Nirew came to be, and she found that this would be his future queen. It tore her world apart. They spent less time together. When she confronted young Aden with these feelings, he pushed her away. He loved Kyya, but as a friend. It was devastating for her. Some days I couldn't get her out of her quarters. She refused bonding with her mother. She stayed away, but on the sunset that his father was killed, Kyya came back for him, and she saw I was in grave danger, she gave her life for me. She loved so much, but that love didn't overtake her real mission in her life. She gave her life to save me. I believe that you are doing the same thing Gina." Dar said with a tear in his eyes.

"I can't possibly be compared to her; she was braver than I could ever be." I said.

"That's where you're wrong. Maggie is your friend, and you came to a place where you could possibly lose your life to save hers, and along this journey you fell in love." Dar said.

"I don't want to say I'm in love with anyone ever again." I said, not wanting to look at him, while he was starring in my direction.

"Gina, the point of my story was she never gave up. Her goal was to protect me, and she did this even though the love of her life wasn't the love of her life?" Dar said.

"So, even though I have feelings for Aden… my goal is to get Maggie, so stay focused on her?" I whispered.

"I would never tell you to kill the love you feel for our King, but remember your first priority, because my daughter Kyya did." Dar wept silently.

"Are you okay Dar?" I asked, touching his shoulder as we walked.

"I shed one tear when I bring up her death. It's my family's tradition." He wiped the tear and continued on as if nothing had ever happened. I couldn't ever just cry one tear if I lost the person whom I was closes with. There was something to Dar, and to all these creatures here. They had families that they genially loved but they couldn't be with. There first priority was to the King, and the next was me and then to their families. I thought I had guilt all over me before, now it felt even worse.

As we made it back to the castle, we walked passed Nirew, her friends and Queen Patano. I tried to walk faster so we did not have to speak. I wanted nothing to do with his queen to be. I didn't want to see Aden again if I didn't have to.

"Being, come and sit down." Nirew snapped her fingers, and I ignored her "Did you not hear me?"

"I am not a dog, so don't snap your fingers at me." I said.

"I heard you travel from Earth, how are you adapting here?" Nirew asked.

"I am getting along just fine." I stared at Dar whom was standing off to the side in a posture of respect towards Nirew.

"Dar, you may excuse yourself." Nirew said to him. He bowed and walked away. "And, your friend…What is her given?"

"Why do you want to know so much about me?" I snapped

"I heard you were a fighter." Nirew and her friends laughed. "Have a seat."Nirew looked human like, skinny, beautiful long black hair. She had the best of jewelry and clothes. Her friends dressed beneath her status, because they were her lackeys. Queen Patano was like a mother to Aden, so she had to be to Nirew. It was all over her face that she couldn't stand Nirew, but I sat down, next to Queen Patano, and stared at Nirew.

"Yeah." I said very agitated.

"I'm just trying to get to know you." Nirew said. "Aden seems to fret if I say one bad thing about you… Not that I have." She smiled.

"She is a wonderful Being." Queen Patano said. I smiled at her and Nirew gave her the dirtiest look.

"Queen Patano, you have taken her under your wing as a daughter?" Nirew asked trying to hide the discomfort in her voice.

"I am fond of Gina, I will admit. But my allegiance is with you Nirew." It pained Queen Patano to say, it was written over her face.

"Being, what is your given?" Nirew asked.

"Gina." I said.

"Why have you been so attached to my Aden when I have been absent?" Nirew asked.

"That is it. That's none of your concern. Good day." I said standing.

"I'm not done with you yet, and you will do good to know your manners. This is not your Earth, and I can throw you to the wild Jals." Nirew snapped. "Now sit down."

"And what would you tell your King. He would surely blow fire out of his….." I said and Queen Patano interrupted.

"Gina!" Queen Patano shook her head no. "I'm sure he would take your head off and feed it to the She-ads." I smiled at Queen Patano and walked away. I heard Nirew and her friends gasp. I walked looking for Aden, and when I found him, I completely went off.

"Look, I know Nirew is going to be your whatever, but tell her not to speak to me, I might have to feed her to alligators." I yelled.

"We do not have alligators." He smiled.

"Well whatever's here that looks like one?" I yelled.

"It is not in our custom to be discourteous Gina." Aden said.

"Well you weren't nice when I first met you." I mocked him.

"Will you calm down?" He asked. "What could she have possibly said that would get under your skin?"

"Tell her to stop asking me question, if she wants any information, get it from you. It's disgusting, how she likes to state her claim over you." I snapped.

"Sounds to me you're a bit resentful." He looked away. "Whoopee, she got her trophy. Tell her to stay away from me." I snapped.

"She's just being indignant because she's becoming worried of our bond we have."

"Had." I corrected him.

"Have." He turned his head towards me.

"As I recall, you will forget I ever existed. So it's had."

"I was angry and needed time. So it's have." He became a little annoyed.

"That's not an apology."

"I'm not making one."

"Whatever! Just keep her away from me." I said with an angry tone because he was so calm.

"I'll take care of it... I'll talk to her...Is that better?" he turned away as I was looking for an indication of what he meant by have. I tried to read him, like he reads me, by the changes in his facial expressions.

"Good!" I said.

"Why don't you ask me what I'm thinking instead of searching for answers in my body language?" Aden asked.

"Ugh! Stop invading my thoughts." I snapped.

"You're standing here looking at me... I'm looking at you... What else am I supposed to do?" He said so arrogantly.

"Read my mind now, what is it saying?" I said giving him so many vulgar words I could think of about how I was feeling about this place.

"That is adolescent of you, especially when you've been treated so nicely." He turned away from me and looked back at me.

"By Dar yes, Queen Patano yes, and Kilen, and Lilar.... But since your pretty princess has arrived you've barely made eye contact with me." I yelled.

"It would be inappropriate." Aden yelled back.

"Would it?" I asked.

"I'm making eye contact now Gina." Aden stepped close to me starring in my eyes. I loved his eyes. I loved... He was reading my thoughts because he withdrew his stare.

"Was that enough eye contact?"

"I think that it was. My king. You must not get fussy with the Being." Nirew stood observing our whole argument.

"Lady Nirew." Aden said.

****

Gina turned to walk away from me. Nirew didn't even glance her way when Gina walked passed her. I watched Lady Nirew just give a smirk. She was very patronizing.

"My King, our guests have arrived." Lady Nirew said. I walked with Lady Nirew towards her guests. I must say I really didn't want to deal with anyone at this moment. We approached the corridor and I noticed that my father's advisors were present. I had no word they were coming. I looked at Lady Nirew because I knew she had invited them, they themselves would have sent word before their arrivals. "Lady Nirew what have you done?" I whispered.

"You will see my king. Welcome Advisors." Lady Nirew bowed.

"Si no vo mek nob be be me sik." Advisor Luviably spoke.

"I had no idea of your arrival or else I would have better prepared." I spoke.

"Lady Nirew has spoken for you." Advisor Won said.

"She feels you are ready to be crowned my prince." Advisor Plantes said.

"When the time is right, I will be." I looked at Lady Nirew who was much pleased. Then I smelt her scent. This was not a good time for her to be visible. A screeching sound, made Lady Nirew drop to her knees. I turned to see Gina covering her ears and being pulled towards us.

"No. Advisors Plantes." I yelled trying to shield Gina. Advisor Plantes raised his hand and pushing me to the side.

"Aden, Soclyninaca." Advisor Won spoke. I instantly froze in place. I struggled to get free, but it was a ritual, that not even I knew how to get out of.

"What is this?" Advisor Plantes asked. "A Being in our world, unleashed." He made a leash appear and wrapped it around Gina's neck. "Obedience." Gina was kneeling on the floor, trying to take the leash from around her, choking.

"Aden. Explain quickly." Advisor Luviably said putting her hand inches from my heart as she closed her eyes. She opens them and they lit with answers of uncertainty and she had searched my heart for answers and found them all. I turned to see Gina whom was at my feet. I hated to see her like that, but I had no control.

"Rise to your feet Lady Nirew." Advisor Plantes spoke. "This is the way the Being shall remain, Prince Aden."

"If I am to be crowned, don't I get a say?" I asked.

"Your father would be devastated if he were here." Advisor Won said. I knew Dar, Kilen and Queen Patano was observing.

"Don't..." I said softly looking at Gina.

"Don't what? Sik nok foolik smok both der." Advisor Luviably yelled.

"Stop moving." I snapped at Gina. I was angry for her being so damn helpless. I was angry with myself.

"Lady Nirew, you spoke nothing of this to us." Advisor Luviably reprimanded her. I felt hopeless trying not to look at Gina. The more she struggled the tighter the leash would be held. She passed out. I never wanted this. I never wanted for Gina to kneel to me. I never wanted her to make me feel like I was more than she was, but in this world I was.

"If I may." Queen Patano approached. "Advisor Luviably, place her hand upon Queen Patano's heart. Then her eyes upon mine." Seconds after Advisor Luviably, looked upon me.

"Mo mok se mur se Advisor Plantes." Advisor Luviably said. "We must seek council alone, now."

I saw Gina on the floor and then the next I was alone in front of the Advisors. They held council far from the findings of anyone in Nexima. You could only see them when they took you to this hidden zone. I stood ready to face whatever they were to place upon me. I was happy that Gina was alright now.

"Why do you think not of Lady Nirew instead of this Being?" Advisor Luviably asked. I said not a word, for whatever answer I gave she would see right through it.

"Prince Aden, you have broken a rule for older than you are. What are we to do? Even though your intentions are noble... How do we explain this to the Elder? For we must answer to him if he gets word and will hold you punishable for breaking the Law even if you are King. You must take your place as king and place us as your Advisors immediately so we can help you." Advisor Won asked.

"I see your future now Prince Aden, it is very uncertain because you have choices to make within you. But this is law... you must not break it." Advisor Plates said.

"I made a promise I intend to keep. I will rescue her friend and she will leave. She did not treat me as you treated her in her world. For whatever my feelings have grown to be, they will dissipate once she leaves. There will be no leash. Whatever the consequences are with the Elder, I will deal with him. For you all have authority until I take my place on the throne." I looked at them.

"Why would you risk so much for one Being?" Advisor Luviably asked? Her eyes glittered with curiosity. She watched me carefully studying me and the way I would answer.

"She has befriended me as I her. If I was to ever return to her world for anything… she would help me." I spoke through my teeth.

"Very well." Advisor Won said. I was standing in my corridor. Lady Nirew awaited me with a remorseful face.

"My king, I do apologize." She bowed.

"If you didn't know about her, what makes you assume they did?" I faced her. "Do not bow. Look at me."

"I know not. I was trying to surprise you." She still looked sadden. I turned from her and walked. "The Being, is she who you search for?"

"Yes." I stopped walking. "Are you alright Lady Nirew?" I looked at her.

"She is in her quarters. You need not fret over me. Go to her." She spoke through her gritted teeth. I looked at her and read her mind She asked did I love this Being? I walked away, not wanting to respond to her thoughts. I walked to Gina's quarters. It seemed so insensitive to leave Lady Nirew, but I needed to see for myself Gina was ok. I entered Gina's room. She lied on the bed with the leash still attached.

"I tried my king, but I cannot remove it." Queen Patano said.

"Shak lok mek mor sor." I said and the leash vanished. You could see that an instance gulp of fresh air went through Gina, but still she lied still. Dar kneeled by her side. He was more upset than I. Lady Nirew walked in and stood by me. She stared at me. I think she knew at that moment Gina meant something to me. She grabbed my hand.

"My king, let Dar have his moment." Lady Nirew said.

I stared at Dar as he waited patiently for a response from Gina as did Queen Patano and Kilen.

For the first time since Gina has been here, I saw the worry on Kilen's face. He was pained. I didn't want to walk away like she said because it was me who wanted to have that moment with her. I stood as Lady Nirew tugged at my arm. That sunset Gina still hadn't opened her eyes. Everyone waited outside her door, Kilen, Ballajamen, and Queen Patano. Lady Nirew had fallen asleep next to me, and I managed to slip out of bed unnoticed. I glided to Gina's door.

"Has she awakened?" I asked Dar, whom was still sadden.

"No, not yet my king." Dar said. Queen Patano, Ballajamen and Kilen stood off to the side. I opened her door and everyone followed me in. I sat in the chair that was place at her side. I glanced at Gina. She was dreaming. It was cluttered at first. I shifted my head, trying to understand the dream, and then it became less chaotic. Gina dreamed that she was with Maggie, and she was telling her things she couldn't say to me they sat at a table in a beautiful restaurant. There were beautiful red and white flowers on the table: "I want to tell him so bad Maggie, but I can't." Gina said. "Maybe it's for the best, maybe he really doesn't love you how you want him to." Maggie said. "I know I give up. I want to go home now." Gina said. "Aden would have told you if he cared for you." Maggie spoke. "No, he never would tell me how he feels do to all the promises he has made, he always kept his feelings to himself.

Some things are just far more important than his own happiness." Gina shedded a tear. "If he loved you nothing else would matter."

"I guess you're right Mag."

"Because, it wasn't meant to be." Maggie said. Gina moved. Her dream rattled me a little bit. She opened her eyes inhaling air and exhaling really fast. She turned over and looked at me.

"Are you alright?" I asked. She said nothing as she sat up. She rubbed her neck.

"Young one. Speak." Dar sat beside her. Gina tried to respond, but she couldn't.

"They have placed a ritual upon her throat; she will be silenced for a day. She will speak by mid-day tomorrow. I'm happy you're all right Gina." I said as I walked out of the room. I was confused about everything at this point. As I slipped back into bed with Lady Nirew, making as if I never left, I descriptively made a Being pro and con list in my head about the two as I struggled to close my eyes and rest. What was more important? I didn't know anymore.

Chapter 13: The Light of Pleasure

I walked into the hallway which was making me sick to do every day. I could barely speak after what happened yesterday. I was walking and waiting. Wondering and being angry. It was all driving me crazy. "Being, you have a lot of concentrated energy trying to detest King Aden right now." Queen Patano said walking behind me in the hallway.

"I hate him, I do."

"Do you? I don't think you do. I think you want to hate him, but you don't." She said.

"He has put me in a position I really hate myself right now." I said in a hoarse voice.

"He didn't know that the advisors would be here." Queen Patano said.

"Who are they anyway?" As the words became clearer in a whisper.

"The advisors are the oldest, wisest leaders to the king of Sawdawa. They are to direct the king on his path and counsel him when he needs it."

"So basically he has charge over them?" I paused. "Why didn't they stop when he told them to? They almost took my head off." The hoarseness in my voice reappeared.

"Until King Aden, physically and willfully takes his place on the throne, they remain in control. Even when he does becomes king they still have charge over him to enforce the laws."

"Well he is king already. They should respect him and listen to him." I said.

"He has little authority now. He has broken a sacred law."

"How is that when they consult him for everything?"

"We consult him for everything, not the advisors." Queen Patano said as Lady Nirew approached us.

"Hello Being." Lady Nirew spoke, and I said nothing. "It was unfortunate what happened the past sunset, but my king will rescue your filthy friend and you two will be on your way." Lady Nirew said..

"Lady Nirew." Queen Patano said.

"As if you weren't aware what would happen?" I said. "I don't want to talk anymore. I will see you later Queen Patano." I walked away.

"Gina, wait!" She said as I stopped.

"Yes, Queen Patano." I said trying to set aside my anger.

"You must not hurt so much. This situation is only complicated for the time being." Queen Patano whispered.

"His allegiance is to her, and so is yours. You both said it. Dar is the only one whose here for me.

Excuse me!" I said.

"I have to be, it's the way it works on Nexima Gina." Queen Patano said trying to comfort me.

"Please excuse me." I walked away.

I went into my room, Dar insisted on talking, but I refused. I was tired of waiting I wanted to get out of here as soon as possible. So I left the castle, climbing out of the window. Dar and Kilen were nowhere around me. This place was horrible I couldn't take being here anymore. I walked a few miles away from the village, and everything was close and it got dark and windy. I walked and walked to clear my head, and when I wanted to turn back, I was lost. I didn't know where to go. I was in a world where I knew no one, and had no knowledge of my direction and how to contact someone for shelter or even food.

I saw a bright light across a field, it seemed as if it was inviting me to come towards it. So I walked through sand and mud. The dress I wore was dirty. I walked until I finally made it to the light which turned out to be a tall male creature. His hair was short and blond. His eyes were blue of the sea water on Earth. He wore no shirt, and his pants were purple. He smiled and grabbed my hands.

"Let's warm you up." He said.

I couldn't speak, the cold, and dirt had me speechless, but it was the light that had me in a trance. I wanted to go deeper into it. When he opened what seemed like a tent, there was nothing, but light. When I entered, there were people everywhere. It seemed like a world inside of a world. There were rooms everywhere, there was an upstairs. These people were trapped on this planet like me. They had their own place.

"You can live out your every fantasy in here. Whatever you want, you can have." He whispered in my ear.

I didn't speak, somehow my mouth couldn't get anything out. This is where I belonged. The humans seemed at peace, with pretty gowns on, some with no gowns, and they were laughing and lying around. Some playing games, and even listening to sweet music. It seemed like a place where no one cared about clothing. The guys stood like little angels with wings, with no clothing. All the women were draped with cloths. "Let's get you cleaned up." The guy smiled, and snapped his fingers, I was clean in no time. I looked at myself standing in a cloth that could easily be taken off with one tug. It was a beautiful short golden cloth that fit around my body like a one piece bathing suit. My body was practically exposed. My hair was curly and long. "Will you relax with me?" The guy asked "Tell me your deepest desire, and I'll make it come true." He leaned in my ear. I looked in his eyes, they sparkled. He traced my neck with his lips without touching me. The closer he came, the more relaxed I felt. The tension faded. The relaxation started, and I laughed. I didn't know why, I was just happy.

****

I sat at the table in the common room. I was talking to Lady Nirew and Queen Patano; I must admit my attention wasn't in that room though I could answer every question directed towards me. Gina and I had exchange various words, and they weren't pleasant. It must have been very devastating to see Lady Nirew. The way Gina had quickly become aggressive was odd, but appealing, no doubt. Lady Nirew, it had been eras, and I truly missed her a time or two. I was too concerned with myself to acknowledge the pain I must have caused her by being away from her. She too was on guard towards Gina. But she knew that she had nothing to fear that I was too loyal to her to even leave her side. Lady Nirew- Gina. There images plastered in my mind standing face to face. When the room shook, my mind cleared. I wondered what was happening. Dar entered the room.

"She's gone?" Dar said.
"Who's gone?" I stood from my seat.
"Gina. She left out of her window."

"What? Why weren't you with her?" I asked.

"I was standing outside of her door. I didn't think she would go out of the window, my king." Dar said bowing with regret.

"How long has she been gone?" I asked.

"My king, I don't know. It could have been more than moments." Dar said.

"Kilen, let's go. Dar you search the village. Get her back here." I yelled.

"Let her go Aden, she doesn't belong here anyway." Lady Nirew said.

"And you, do you think you belong here anymore than she?" I snapped.

"Excuse me?" Lady Nirew stood up "Ever since that Being has been here you have been a different person Aden. What is wrong with you?" I said nothing.

"I apologize to you Lady Nirew, I made a promise I intend on keeping. And to do that I must get her back here." I said as Lady Nirew walked towards me.

"You and your promises, must you be so noble my king?" Lady Nirew said, as she lightly laid her lips across mine.

"I will search too my king." Queen Patano said. I could hear the disgust in her mind. We all went separate ways I went to the end of the village. I search through everything, every place I could find. I didn't know where she could be. I would hate myself if something happened to her. Dar spoke through his mind, it was a rare gift he had. "A dweller said she went to the tents. Towards the light."

"What tent, what light?" I asked.

"It can only be seen at night. Prince Griven tents, in the sands." Kilen said.

"Damn it! I need you and a handful of guardsmen to get here Dar."

"We can't get there, its work hours, and it's going to be too many people to get through. Villagers will be scared." Dar said.

"Come at sunset." I said "What is wrong with her?" I whispered.

"Shall I answer, or do you wish to speak with yourself?" Kilen asked.

"Let's not talk; I know what you are going to say."

"I doubt that my king. Gravity is pulling you two together, but you both keep pushing each other away. That's what's wrong with this situation." Kilen said.

I sat on the edge of the sands. I knew it was a rare occasion that Kilen spoke, but when he did, he got straight to the point, and wouldn't sugar coat anything. Dar and a few soldiers made it as soon as sunset hits. I had to get Gina out of there. It was bothering me, she was that angry to leave. We waited, and waited for the light to shine. The light trapped any skin that was powerless, and couldn't avoid it.

We all crept up on the tent, which seem to be farther than what it was. When we arrived, I opened the tent, and sand demons stood angry. I saw Gina laughing. She seemed to have a great time, but that was the light, that's what it did, made you feel good, it was like a drug. She was hardly dressed. Dar stood next to Gina. She was out of it; she probably had laughed and had been consumed for a long time.

"Well, well, well. Mr. Aden Bartarino." What are you doing here?" Prince Griven said standing up.

"I'm here to get my keep." I said.

"She's no longer yours. She wears anger on her sleeves, and she has relinquished herself." He said. "Isn't that right my love?" he showed a leash around her neck and he caressed Gina's face.

"Get your hands off her." I became angry that he could do that effortlessly.

"Does it upset you prince Aden? That I can touch her and do almost anything with her." Prince Griven laughed.

"Dar!" I said.

"She's mine. She came willingly." Prince Griven stood behind Gina, caressing her neck, as she smiled. It sickened me.

"She can't think straight with this light, and you know it." I snapped.

"It's too late. She has dance, and has been better company for me than anyone, which means, she stays. You know the rules. If….you can get her out of the trance, then she's yours." He said.

"Gina, let's go." I whispered walking over to her, but she laughed, "Gina, snap out of it damn it." I yelled.

"Looks like she's mine." Prince Griven said walking around laughing and taunting. Like he knew best.

"She will die, and you know it. If she stays in this light." I snapped.

"Well, save her from death." Prince Griven yelled. "Isn't it your job Aden? To be the best like daddy wanted." He mocked. "Save her Aden, Save her!"

"Gina, can you hear me?" I asked. She didn't respond, but she swayed as if there were music on.

"Tick tock." Prince Griven laughed sipping out of his golden goblet. The only thing I could think of was whispering in her ear, "Maggie needs you, let's go home." She shook her head trying to come to, she recognized the name, but she wouldn't budge... So I tried repeating it, and she was slowing coming out of the trance the light had her in. Finally I said, "Let me take you and Maggie home, Gina." I said as Gina opened her eyes.

"What's going on?" Gina asked.

"No, no. no! It's not fair." Prince Griven smiled and waved his hands of dismissal. "I'm bored go away."

"Let's get out of here." Dar snatched Gina and before we could leave the tent the Demons stood around us. It was Dar, Kilen, five guardsmen and I.

"No, you just don't get her that easy. I wish to play a game with you Aden." Prince Griven said.

"What kind of game?" I said just then I slid an emerald blade out of my pocket.

"No." Prince Griven rose above us on top of sand "You have had your way for far too long Aden." The sand lifted me from the ground, Gina was still trying to get out of the light trance, but she couldn't. "I want you to sign over your country."

"You know that will never happen." I said struggling to get free from the sand grasp around my neck.

"This is not a battle you want with me."

"And why not? I am not afraid of Aden. I never have been, and never will be." Prince Griven said.

"You must admit jealousy runs deep in your family." I managed to get the words out. "Aden, Aden! I love a challenge, but right now I have the upper hand." Prince Griven laughed.

"So why, are you going to be defeated once again?" I said.

"You're little army you have with you now, can be wiped out in seconds. Your little princess will die, while you hang from my pet." Prince Griven said as sand hand gripped my neck tighter to get free. Kilen and Dar fought the demons. Blood dripped from Gina's mouth because all she did was laugh. She spun herself around in a circle. Sand flew around as Prince Griven laughed. A dagger flew through the sand that gripped me and I fell. I ran towards Prince Griven, but he disappeared along with his demons.

We made it over the sands. Gina had come out of the trance, and she didn't know what was going on. She was coughing up blood and wiping it from her mouth. She walked in silence, but I was angry. "What is wrong with you?" I yelled.

"What's wrong with you?" She yelled back trying to cover herself.

"It's insane for you to wonder around a place you've never been when you know Beings are outlawed here?" I stopped.

"Aden as if you care." She walked away.

"Don't walk away from me. Do you despise me that much that you would get yourself killed?" I yelled "Look at you. You're barely dressed."

"I hate you." She cried.

"Why because of one discrepancy?" I asked her.

"You use me, you played with my emotions." Gina yelled.

"Prince Griven just used you."

"What did he do?" She looked at me.

"I wasn't there. You're naked practically. They use skins for amusement in any way they see fit." I pulled out the cloak I had given her, and handed it to her. She quickly covered herself.

"Great now I was use by two people." She cried.

"I didn't use you."

"You did. You can't even justify it." She wiped her eyes. We stood for a minute and she walked away crying.

"Just because of a kiss? Hey you pushed that on me, I didn't ask for it. You kept coming around. I asked for nothing but solitude."

"Oh, wow, you could have walked away for one. Two, I wish I stayed away from you."

"Stop crying. You cry way too much, for a person who's…?" I said losing control of myself and this situation.

"Who's what? Stupid for trying to be a friend with someone who needs help with life and then falling for him even though he will get married? A user." She yelled.

"Fine, I used you. Believe it, and I can't wait to get married and get you out of this world. Does that make you feel better?" I followed behind her. Dar, Kilen and the guardsmen kept their distance from us, while we argued.

"No." She turned around and punched me, I quickly stumbled back. "That makes me feel better." Her knuckles burned from touching me, and she shook her hand from the pain, she pulled the leash from around her neck as Dar quickly ran to her aid. He wrapped her hand.

"What was that for? That was really unnecessary." she ignored me and walked away. I had to admit that was a good throw.

Dar grabbed her, covered her with a cloak and we all walked back in silence. They kept us separated. There was more discussed in front of Kilen and the others than needed to be, but no one wanted to say anything. We arrived to the castle, and Lilar ran towards me, and said the medicine is complete.

"Good." I said looking at Gina.

"Great." She replied and walked away.

Lady Nirew looked at me and asked "What was that about?"

"Nothing. She's just ready to leave." I said walking away.

"Thank goodness." She followed me. There was nothing left to say. Gina hated me, now I hated her. She didn't want to understand me, and I refused to understand her. Nexima is where my heart must be not with Gina. I was once all confused, but not anymore.

Chapter 14: Announcement

"Queen Patano, is there a way for me to talk to Maggie to see what's going through her mind?"

"Gina there is a way, and only one person who can do it, but I'm afraid he won't." Queen Patano said.

"Who?" I asked.

"Dar. He is one of the elders of the skins. He has the power to transmit, and obtain messages through dreams. Unfortunately, when he was captured by the lead She-ad, Ponchopalapare, he absorbed some of his abilities. That's how he got through to you. Dar doesn't like to do it because it's dangerous."

"Why is it so dangerous?" I sat indulging in the conversation.

"It's dangerous for you and Maggie. You two are human Beings, not Skins. Your minds are delicate and you use only a little capacity of it. As for Skins they use a thousand times more than a Being." Queen Patano said.

"What do you mean? I thought Skins were Beings."

"Flesh on outside, no spirit or soul inside, just brains. They know what's going on in people minds worlds away. That's why they are born to be kept by kings and queens of our world. Just as Beings"

"Maggie was awake in my dream; do you think she still is?" I asked.

"If she has awakened, it is at his will. The poison still runs deep in her, and she only has a little while before she dies. I must go, the King and Lady Nirew awaits my arrival." She lifted my face so that my eyes could meet hers. "Fear not child, our King will do everything in his power to make you happy, you are his concern rather you believe it or not. Until he can, have a little assurance in your God that you told me so much about." She smiled and strutted away.

"How can you be so sure, I mean….?" I asked.

"It's written over his face." She disappeared. I walked to this room with the big window that has this bench sitting directly in front of it. I wore my dingy old shirt and sweats I had on when I first come to this new world. I was happy not to be in silk dresses for once and to have my hair pint in a ponytail. I was being normal me, the only thing that was missing was Maggie. The sun shined through the window so brightly, and it was warm on my skin. It was the first time the weather was warm instead of cold in this world. All I thought about was seeing Maggie smile. Tears quickly erupted from my eyes. I felt like I had torn down two worlds to where they can't be repaired. I burst into a loud cry. I couldn't hold it together anymore. I had to let it out, somewhere in peace and by myself. Somewhere I could blame myself and no one would try and cheer me up. I needed to release it so I could move on. I hurt Aden, Maggie and I was ruining Lady Nirew's life by sending her one true love somewhere to die. I cried out loud for the second time thinking and repeating I know they hated me, and how much I was sorry, but this time it was loud enough to release the pain. For one moment, I felt the room get warmer, I hugged my knees tighter and cried. I wanted no one around. Aden's aura was in that room for a long time. He stood and said nothing. He kept his distance.

"I don't hate you Gina." Aden approached me.

"Don't, go be with your, whatever she is." I said hugging my knees tighter.

"My concern is you at this moment. I don't want you to feel guilty of anything." Aden said standing next to me. Just then Queen Patano words ran through my mind.

"Aden, I'm hurting. I messed up so much." I cried.

"Gina…. Life is not always easy. And it surely doesn't turn out the way we want it. I know this." He said looking in my eyes. "You love your God, and you talk to him constantly. Don't you have faith everything will be okay?" He looked so concerned that I kept crying.

"You don't understand how I feel right now." I turned from him.

"I do. I can feel your pain and have experienced a lost. It pains me every day." He walked to the window. "And it's sad to say, I will experience another…."

"What do you mean?" I walked towards him, standing at his side.

"Things are complicated. People…. complications are everywhere. Every day we lose those we know, or have heard of. It gets harder, not easier." He looked at me as I still cried. "I wish, that I… could make… somehow make this pain fade from you."

"Don't worry about it, I'll cry and get it over with." I said as the tears ran continuously.

"I have to show you something." He said.

I faced him, and he lifted a finger, where the tears ran down my face. He pushed the tip of his finger to the tears, and they evaporated. All I felt was warmth. I closed my eyes as he did them one by one. I opened my eyes, and his face was turned towards the door way. "How did you do that?" I asked.

"Practicing, for a moment like this. You shed many tears, and I feel hopeless at times because I cannot take your sorrows away." He stared at me and his eyes commanded that I believed his words.

"Why do you make me want you and then you pull away… all the time?" I said as our faces were close enough I could feel his breath on my lips.

"Complication." He said.

"Only because of you're making them."

"I would change things if I could."

"Aden, why don't you do it then?" He moved closer, and he closed his eyes. His lips were a space from mine.

"Because I can't." He opened his eyes and looked at me. I wanted to just kiss him, I didn't care. Screw the rules, screw the laws, I wanted to burn. I wanted to at this moment. I wanted to feel the pain, just to focus on something else, besides my hurt. "Don't substitute pain for pain." He still stood close.

"Aden, do you love me?" He stood in silent. His eyes stared into mine. He was thinking, but he said nothing. "It's not complicated to answer that question." Tears still ran down my face.

"It's complicated."

"No it's not."

"I want to show you something else."

"What?" He lifted his hands and put them next to my chest, far enough he wouldn't hurt me.

"Close your eyes." I closed my eyes. He whispered something. A phrase I did not understand. It was in his language. "Mockloha ma-me-so-tru." After he whispered these words. Suddenly he had me pulled close to him and we were kissing. The kiss was passionate as he held me so tight. It was like he had been holding this in for a while, we both were. I tried to pull away to question it, but I was locked in. Suddenly, the feeling stopped. It had been an image in my mind. It wasn't real.

"What was that?" I was flustered.

"That's what you needed. Something to take home with you."

"But how?" When I stared at him, he looked away from me. I looked and there stood Lady Nirew.

"Lady Nirew!" He said. She stormed off, and he followed her. I had done it again.

****

I searched for Lady Nirew. She was in my quarters gazing out of the window. I walked in slowly, and tried to read her mind, but she had the ability to block that. She turned towards me, but still said nothing. I knew I had to correct this situation too, but I knew not what to say. I stood next to her and grabbed her hands.

"My King, do you love not I anymore." Lady Nirew asked.

"Lady Nirew, don't question my affection for you." I replied.

"I have waited so patiently my king… eras, just to come back and see you have fallen in love with a Being. An outlawed creature."

"I didn't mean for you to find anything troublesome for me calming Gina."

"It shouldn't even have an attachment to you. It is beneath us and it should be leashed. But you fight so hard against that law. Why my king? I do not understand."

"She was kind to me in her world. She befriended me…. and I have grown fond of her friendship." I said.

"It has turned to be a kinship like Kyya. Hasn't it?" She asked. "Tell me the truth. You love her don't you?"

"I will not speak of Kyya with you." I grew a little guarded dropping her hands.

"So, it has?" Lady Nirew followed me around as I walked. "Do you perhaps feel the same for this Being?"

"There is no need for spitefulness. I will marry you as planned." I said even though some parts of me felt deeply about Gina as she did of me. Did Nirew know this? Why did she want to force me to answer?

"Oh! Aden!" Lady Nirew said hugging me. "I knew you would never choose anyone other than me."

"Prepare for the day Lady Nirew. I will see you soon." I smiled.

I couldn't tell Lady Nirew anything I might feel for Gina. I had to bury those feelings deep down inside me. I had to take them to my Urn. I knew what I had to do. I knew what Nexima laws were. Gina would be gone after her friend would be rescued and my life will continue as king of this world. I walked through the halls. It was too calm and quiet. It's usually all types of noise. The noise comprise of servers walking by with their so-called version of tip-toe across the floors and cooks preparing food in the kitchen. Guardsmen strutting up and down the hallways, messengers flying in and out. I was getting very curious. I had perfect hearing, vision that is impeccable, and a nose that can pick up any distinct smell. I heard footsteps that weren't to far away. The shoes seem like the type guardsmen's wore, but not mine. I smelled dripping blood, and burnt emerald blades. The center of the hallway was empty. I was in the open looking as I heard steps then a scream, I couldn't tell if it was Gina, or Nirew. Then another scream. It was close. Seconds later I was knocked down. I tried to jump up, but I was knocked backed down. I glided across the floor, and stood up.

I prompt myself in my stance, trying hard to follow the footsteps and smell, but it wasn't helping me. Something was tossed in my eyes, so I was paralyzed by my senses; the only thing I could rely on now was being a phantom. I stood still. "Malsa Dana" I said. I felt my senses kick straight in, only through my eyes. I could zoom on everything. It was two phantoms in the rooms, a skin, and ten guardsmen. There was a double attack. I was able to counter it. My hands lit, and I tossed fire quickly.

I felt the power of the two phantoms toss me against the wall. I was attacked over and over again by them but I was able to attack the guardsmen, but not the phantom. I began to get mad and I attacked first this time, until I recognized Kilen, Ballajamen and Dar. Kilen knew it and they stopped their attack.

"What are you doing?" I asked out of breath.

"Training. You are out of step, my king." Kilen said, blowing dust from my eyes so I could see.

"Without telling me." I was bent over.

"If you're attacked by She-ads, they will not warn you first, my king." Dar said.

"My senses was off, how come I didn't sense you in the beginning?" I asked.

"You were distracted." Kilen said.

"Guardsmen shoes seemed far away?" I looked around.

"Ritual of distance." Dar said.

"Dripping blood?" I asked still calming my breath.

"Westtels blood?" Dar added.

"Ritual of distraction." Kilen said.

"Screams?" I starred at them.

"Ritual of aggression. Which you did not fall for…why?" Queen Patano said approaching.

"I heard two screams, I couldn't detect whom it was." I said.

"That was why you had a slow reaction." Queen Patano said looking at Kilen, and Dar.

"Enough talk."Kilen said disappearing and Dar seconds later, and so did the guardsmen.

"Good luck, my king." Queen Patano said gliding away.

"And the training begins." I said disappearing, knocking Kilen and Dar back visible. I slid tripping all the guards in a circle. I knew my biggest competition was Kilen and Dar so I had to take the guards out first. Elder Phantoms had tricks I knew nothing about. So did Elder Skins. Ballajamen was a piece of cake. Once the guards were out of the picture I appeared and attacked Ballajamen. He was the simplest to get next. When I attacked Dar it wasn't him, they were using more rituals. They attacked me, and I was getting banged up. An emerald blade cut me a few times.

"Careless. Wake up Aden." Dar yelled.

I glided in a circle, "Ceralas." I said making dirt appear. I slid, "Sapras Lavas." I added with my arms stretched open in front of me, making a loud thunderous sound to split through the armor of rituals they had lined up for me. It was something they didn't know I knew. It was a ritual to paralyze rituals for thirty seconds. Dar and Kilen stood watching, but quickly had a counter attack. Both knocking me down.

"Aden you must move swiftly. You are a phantom. You move like and elderly Being." Kilen yelled as we trained.

"He will try everything to bring you down." Dar said.

"I will. I haven't had training in numbers like this, with so much strength." I yelled humped over, just then Kilen went through me and straighten my posture.

"Stand straight. No break." He flew out of me.

Dar attacked me from behind. I quickly flipped him from my back and flew through the air bouncing off the walls into attack mode on Kilen. Ballajamen threw daggers and stars, I became translucent as two daggers went through me, and two stars cut my arms. Ballajamen ran towards me, I stood still with my arms in a locking position, but he pushed me into the wall. Dar picked me up with his bottom two arms and beat me with his top two fists. "Are you going to let him beat you like this, Aden?

When he did this when he killed your father?" Ballajmen said. I became angry, and my hands burst with fire and flung Dar backwards. I twisted in circles flinging fire from my body, grunting with anger. I took a shape of a tornado of fire, stopping, and everyone stared at me.

"You did it!" Kilen said.

"What? Don't stop now. The fun is just beginning." I said. "You are live fire." Dar said moving from in front of a mirror. I saw myself, there was no skin in sight. I walked up to the mirror and I didn't recognize myself. It was evident, that when I became angry, it was like a switch to this new side of me. I stood paralyzed in the mirror because I saw myself the way my father looked when he died. It was weird and even scary; it could be my last days here. This showed me I needed to be honest with myself and with those around me.

After my training Lady Nirew and I were talking, she was upset I was going on this mission, and she wanted to get married as soon as possible. She wanted to carry on the name Bartarino if I happened to not make it back from the battle.

"Aden, please, just do this for me." Lady Nirew said.

"Why can't you wait until I get back?" I asked her. "We will do the proper ceremony, and when I come back we will marry."

"Will you come back? This isn't a game. This is far beyond your control. You're dealing with a murderer my king." Lady Nirew yelled.

"I know this Lady Nirew. I've gotten all my abilities together. I know I can beat him." I replied.

"Why do you make this so difficult for me?" She pouted.

"I'm not making it difficult; I want you to believe that I will be back. Just show me you have a little faith in me."

"Faith? What is this you speak of?" She asked.

"On Earth, this is what they say to inspire you to believe in God." I said.

"Well, you are my God. I have faith in you, but I cannot have faith in what you are about to do. It seems this Being rescue mission means more to you than I."

"It's not just about her. I mean this thing killed my father, and he will pay for that." I yelled.

"I want to marry you, and if you don't want to marry me, let me know and I'll walk away."

"Don't give me an ultimatum. I didn't say I didn't want to marry you, but I said not now. If you cannot wait, then that means you are selfish and you are full of greed." I walked away from her.

"My king, I am simply saying... I don't want to lose you." Lady Nirew stopped me in the hallway, grabbing me by the arm.

"I know this. I will be fine." I said.

"Do you promise me you will come back?" Lady Nirew said.

"I will not make promises I'm not sure I can keep." I stared into her eyes.

"You are my love, do you know that?" She kissed me.

"And you are mine." I turned to walk and Gina was standing behind me.

"Excuse me." Gina said.

"It is quite alright Being." Lady Nirew said.

"Good Sunrise." I said. I starred at Gina, whom seems to take her glance off me, but said say in her mind. If Nirew was what I wanted, she would let it be.

"Same to you." She walked away, without a word.

I hadn't seen Gina since this sunrise. She was really upset and hurting last night. I watched her as she beat herself down for everything that was going on, and then to see me embraced with Lady Nirew. If anyone knew the story it would be Gina's fault, but it was more at hand here. It was fate as Dar called it. She and I were meant to meet, it was just unfortunate the negative things that happened along the way of our meeting. I walked the hallways looking for her; Dar said that Ballajamen had taken her to the garden in the back.

I stood watching Gina from afar, she was playing with Putterball. She had grown attached to a few people in this world…Dar, Queen Patano, and Putterball. She and I never became the best of anything. I could've spent more time with her, I could've been her friend, but I would be lying about just wanting to be her friend. Lady Nirew and my world were factors of that issue between us. Gina turned and waved smiling. I waved back. Her hair danced with the warm breeze coming off the water, she was in her clothes she wore when I swore to rescue her friend, when I pleaded for her to stay with me to be safe. Gina approached me, with the biggest smile.

"Hey Aden." She said.

"Ballajamen take a break. I'll keep her company for a while." I said. He glided away as Putterball followed behind him.

"What are you doing out here?" she asked.

"I was looking for you." We walked through the garden.

"Don't worry. I'm okay, your life is here?" she smiled. This confused me a bit.

"This is surprising to hear." I stopped walking, staring at her.

"What did you expect? I can't force you into anything. I'm looking forward to seeing Maggie and getting home. To my life." Gina said walking further ahead.

"You are a different person from prior sunsets." I said as I watched her smell flowers. "Seeing you two, kiss and say you love each other… it was enough for me to let go." She giggled nervously. "An eye opener."

I said nothing; I tried to read her mind to see if she was lying. But she was ok with the way things were. It panics me. I didn't know how to take her knew behavior. So I watched her as she sat on the pavement. Her hair blew in the wind. Her scent was still appealing, but I was seeing her in a new light.

"Gina… what happens if Maggie doesn't make it back?" I said sitting next to her.

"I would try to live without her." She smiled a little. "But I know she will make it."

"If she doesn't, would you leave here." I asked avoiding her stare.

"Yes! I couldn't stay here. I mean, it's beautiful, but you will still break laws with me being here." She looked towards the sun. "I'll always remember Dar, Queen Patano, Kilen, and…You!"

"What if I asked you to stay?" I looked at her.

"Never…" I laughed. "No offense. I love your home, but Lady Nirew and I would never get along. I want to go home."

"Oh, I see." I said as her thoughts slipped and she thought about how she loves me to much to impede my destiny. Then she hummed a tune out loud. "What is that you sing?"

"It's a hymn. It's my favorite church song."

"It's very beautiful." I said looking towards the sun as I sat on the pavement next to her. "There will be a ceremony on the marriage. I'm prolonging it until I get back."

"Why not marry her first? She loves you. I mean, what's stopping you?" Gina asked.

"Honestly!" We sat in the garden, "I don't want to right now."

"Don't lead her on, tell her." She said.

"I did, she's not happy about it. Everyone in Nexima is waiting on an announcement from me today, to tell them we are to be wed, and that I have accepted the responsibility of being king. I'm not sure if I want to say we are or we aren't or I am, or I'm not."

"Wow! That's hard."

"Aden, my king let's get you ready." Lady Nirew came in and put her arm around me.

"All right. I will speak with you soon Gina." I walked away along with Lady Nirew.

"Why were you in the garden with her?" Lady Nirew asked walking with me to our quarters.

"We were conversing as I do with most." I said.

"Just stay away from it. Beings are filthy and I don't want you around her." Lady Nirew said.

"Do not do that." I stopped looking at her.

"Do what?"

"Being spiteful, I dislike that."

"You give me every reason to be spiteful of that thing. You concentrate too much on it." She smiled waving to guest.

"Her name is Gina."

"Pardon me, but I don't care my king. I want you to make the announcements so we can get married. I can't wait until she leaves." She kept smiling at guest.

"We will marry when I get back. I'm giving them the same answer I gave you. Please respect that."

"My king, I have waited eras for you. And you will make me wait more?" She snapped.

"Nirew!" I yelled. "When I return, I don't care if I'm filthy and limbs are hanging from my body, we will marry. I'm finished with this conversation." I walked away.

This was very frustrating, because I wanted to give Nirew what she wanted, and I wanted to give Gina what she wanted, but what did I want? I couldn't think. I was doing things for everyone, except me. I had made so many promises. I was ready to keep them all. But there was being king. My decisions will still not be for me, it would be for Nexima. I force myself like Gina forced herself, not to feel for me anymore.

****

I sat in the garden looking at the beautiful flowers. Orange, blues, and purples were common in his garden. Some looked like ice sickles and star shapes. It was wonderful with smells of bake goods. Some with the smell of vanilla aroma. This was a perfect scene from a famous person garden. I walked back to my room, and when I made it there I closed the door and sat. There was a knock at the door, and it burst opened. In strolled Lady Nirew in her beautiful clothes, and her pulled back hair. She stood in front of me with a pathetic grin on her face. She threw one of her hands on her hips.

"Why don't you get up Being and find something to wear. My husband to be is making our engagement official to the world, and you should attend." Lady Nirew said.

"No thanks, I can hear from in here." I said.

"No, no. You should be in the front." She said.

"Why does it matter if I come or not?" I asked.

"It matters because you need to see he loves me and not you."

"Whatever." I stood and tried to walk passed her, but she grabbed me. I tried to pull away from her, but she held on.

"Get off of me." I pushed her face, and scratched her, she let go of me.

"How dare you place your hands upon me?" She said looking at me.

"What's wrong with your face?" Her face looked as if it was ripped. Her skin hung like a sore that had been split open.

"You can get all your ideas of trying to come between us out of your head." Lady Nirew said holding her face.

"I don't have any ideas about Aden. You need to get out of here." I said.

"Good because you can't have him. I will do everything I have to keep him. And I mean anything." She threw something on the bed. "See you soon." She said.

Lady Nirew walked out after leaving a leash on the bed. I didn't like her; I wish I could hang her with this leash. It was something that wasn't right about her, I could feel it in my bones, but my focus was on our long journey tomorrow, to rescue Maggie. I had a lot to fill her in on. On this whole new world I discovered. She will want to kill me. She will give me a lecture about staying away from guys that wants to be left alone. It makes me smile just to want to listen to her complain at me. It's better than hearing utter silence. But of course, if she doesn't make it, I will forever be plagued with getting her killed. My life will be forever changed no matter what. I decided to get dress and try to get myself to enjoy the festivities. I sat out on the side of the castle on a bench. A lot of creatures gathered to hear their king speak. It seemed to be taking him a long time to come to the balcony to give his grand lecture. It was a beautiful day, I stood and look towards the stream in the back of the castle.

"Can I ask you a question?"

"Yes!" I said not even looking back. Aden stood on the side of me.

"What will happen to us if I go through with this?" Aden asked.

"There is no us. This is your world, and my world is Earth. You stay here, I go home." I said as his hair blew in the wind. His crown sat on his head lopsided.

"I don't want you to have hatred for me." Aden lifted his hand to touch me, but he knew what would happen if he did, so he pulled away. It was a feeling I long to feel again. I would kill for it.

"I don't." I turned towards him and fixed his crown straight. "Go make your speech. We have a long journey before I leave." I smiled and this time he returned one. I guess no one understands us more than each other. He knew he had to do the right thing, I knew I had to let him do the right thing; even though I couldn't stand Lady Nirew. My journey with this world was nearly over. I wanted to get back to a normal life. How could I have a normal life without someone I loved? It was inevitable, I had to. It seemed to take forever before the trumpets sound, and every creature sang in harmony. Although I didn't understand it, it was beautiful. Aden and Lady Nirew appeared, and everyone bowed. Dar and Kilen stood next to me. Aden had a glow surrounding him. He knew he was in his element, this is what he was destined to be, a king of a country. A country he loved a country his father loved and was a king of. He stood in white silk, his circlet was a beautiful gold painted porcelain, and his soon to be queen stood by his side. She seems so out of place. I imagined myself next to him, but I wanted to be no queen. They waved. Cheers poured out from everywhere. Then it became quiet. I've never seen a place that could have absolute silence. You could hear the stream in the distance. You could hear chirps from animals, but no one talked or uttered a sound.

"I know, I've been absent from Nexima for a while, but I assure you there will be no more of that. It has taken me many eras to realize my importance here, and I have come to fulfill my destiny. This means, protecting you all from evil that stands on the far end of the walls of Sawdawa. I am here today to tell you that there will not be a marriage ceremony until after the war." Everyone gasp! She looked like her world had fallen apart. She stepped closer to him. She looked embarrassed. "There will be a war and everyone needs to know that. We can't celebrate when there is danger arising. I am ready to claim my crown. I feel there is much more to be learned." As Aden talked I noticed skin hanging from Nirew's arm. It seemed like burnt skin underneath. I just stood there. I moved closer to get a better view, and Nirew turned towards me and followed my gaze, and bent her arm another way. She gave me a nasty look. Something was different about her. Something that no one was paying attention to. I realized she was strange, but what? Everyone was happy to finally to hear from there king. They were really upset to hear that there would be no celebration just yet. Aden began telling how he would assemble his armed forces for a battle. He lists all his plans in full details. Everyone listened until he finished and then the festivities started outside in the village because Aden promised a victory. There were a lot of talking in the hallway of the castle between Nirew and Aden. He tried many times to calm her, but she wanted him to say nothing. He assured her that the marriage would happen, but now wasn't the time. She refuse to understand him, in fact she yells she waited years for them to finally be married, and he apologized a thousand times, but she took her servants and left and vowed never to returned until he had made up his mind about what he wanted, and she yelled her or that disgusting Being. She slammed the door as hard as she could. The door was taller than her and I put together, and it weighed a ton. I couldn't see how she had so much strength. I stood behind the wall, hiding trying not to be seen.

"I know you're there." Aden turned towards the wall.

"Sorry." I said still not revealing myself.

"Do you always ease-drop?" He asked.

"No. I didn't mean to. I didn't want to walk by and have her yelling at me." I walked in plain sight.

"King Aden, Lilar and Queen Patano need you." Ballajamen bowed.

"I will catch up with you later." I said.

"I will meet you in your quarter's later Gina." Aden said walking off.

I had become hopeful again about Aden, but he did promised to marry her. My heart couldn't bare more heartache. I wondered if she would come back and cause chaos. Aden wanted me to stay, but he wanted to make everyone happy and I would not be the one he forces to be happy. He needed to choose what he wanted to do with his life. I would crawl in a corner and die if he'd just tell me he loved me. But he doesn't at all.

****

It was late the night before we were setting out to save Maggie. I sat in the dark in Gina's room waiting for her to walk in. She entered her room wearing my cloak, and lay in the bed. She didn't remove it, she wrapped herself in it. I don't know why I felt like this would be the only time I would be alone with her again. She stared at the wall. She didn't feel my presents yet. I made my way to her bed, and she still didn't move. I stood at the foot of her bed, and she lay on her back. "I knew you were there." She said sitting up.

"Why didn't you speak?" I asked her.

"This is routine, you usually scare me… I say I was thinking I would die." She laughed. "Are you checking on me?"

"Yes." I lied.

"I will miss your presents when you leave." I said.

"Aden!" She faced me. But I stepped out of her view.

"Are you going to forget this place when you go home?"

"You will never let that happen." She laughed.

"I can't come back there you know that, don't you?"

"Why?" She sat up on her arm, and her hair fell in her face.

"I can't leave these people. Once I defeat Ponchopalapare, someone else will try and attack here always."

"Well, I guess tomorrow will be it."

"You say that so easily." I laughed.

"It is now, but I'm sure it won't be tomorrow." She giggled. "Can I ask you something?"

"Where are we at, five-hundred now?"

"Five-hundred what?"

"That's how many questions you've asked."

"Let's go for six-hundred." She smiled.

"What's the question?" I came closer to the bed. Her thoughts instantly went to the day I used the ritual to kiss her. I can't believe I used a ritual on a Being. It could have horrible consequences. I was giving into her wants a lot lately.

"I can't."

"I know. I wish that… just for a moment we could just to say goodbye." She said.

"Words are more powerful." I said standing in front of her. I noticed a leash with Nirew initials on it.

"I don't think so." She gasped.

"What I want to say is……" Grabbing the leash.

"Aden? What's wrong?" She said.

"I have to leave." I said.

"Why?"

"Nirew is looking for me." I left quickly. I appeared seconds behind her whom was wondering the halls. "Nirew."

"Where have you been?" She asked.

"I was wondering the halls as I always do." I said and walked further away from Gina's room.

"Where you with it again?" Nirew asked. She seemed very agitated.

"Yes, to see if she was comfortable." I said.

"Where is Dar? Why isn't he tending to the pup?" She said.

"He asked to go see his family. I lent him the night."

"Where's Kilen?" Lady Nirew asked.

"What is this?" I showed her the leash.

"I…. have no words, for my dishonorable behavior." She looked away.

"I asked you to be kind, not to taunt, and not to be spiteful. And you went behind my back and did it anyway.

"I apologize to you my king, but she is causing a rift between us." Nirew snapped.

"You are causing that rift, not her." I yelled.

"And how so? By trying to keep you focused on what's important…us, and not her and her poor soul of a pup that's captured." She yelled back.

"What if you were in her position? Would you want her to act this way?" I said, and Nirew did not respond. "If you do not act accordingly, we will have another dishonorable thing done, on my behalf." I walked away.

Chapter 15: Treachery

The next morning arrived and it was time to go save Maggie. We were to set off in a few hours. I dressed in my new clothing that a villager personally made for me. They were like sweats but they were of course silk. They had pretty beading, and flower prints. The top was long sleeve with beautiful stitching in it. I was walking through the hallway looking for Dar and Queen Patano, but instead a new guard stood. It was kind of out of the usual for Aden. The guard looked young, handsome and in his thirties, maybe. He looked more like a human than anyone around here. He stood posted and move not even an inch. He wasn't scary at all, so I wasn't afraid to approach him.

"Hi, have you seen Dar?" I asked.

"He has been ordered to another post Gina." He said.

"Thanks…wait, who are you?" When I asked that question he grabbed my arm and snatched me. We flew to the top of the ceiling, and I screamed for Aden. No one came running, but Kilen. He flew to the ceiling and he tried to rescue me, but this guy was too fast.

"Aden." I screamed. Kilen still fought, he punched the guy and I fell from his grip. I was falling and he was fighting. I was screaming, and I knew I was about to hit the porcelain floor hard.

In a matter of time I was caught before I hit the ground. I turned to look, and it was Aden. I screamed from my flesh burning. He quickly sat me down and flew towards the top and fought this creature. It was so fast, and so poised. It quickly changed from a Skin to a beast that crawled on the walls.

Aden pulled a small object out and threw it, and it stuck deep in the creature. It screeched from pain. I watched frantic trying to rub the sting out of my waist, hiding behind a post in the middle of the floor. I couldn't believe what just happened. For whatever reason, things were becoming more difficult than before. Kilen disappeared, as Aden threw these small objects repeatedly and then, Ballajamen and Kilen appeared holding the creature down. They brought him to the ground, and he looked as if he were dead.

"Take him to the tower and lock him there until I get there. Do not leave him alone." Aden said as Ballajamen and Kilen flew off. And vanished into thin air.

"Thank you." I said, Aden glanced at me and walked pass me.

"What's wrong with you?" He still said nothing.

"Oh, you're giving me the silent treatment? Whatever... Where is Dar?" He said nothing; he walked and looked in doorways and rooms.

"Aden!" I said. "Aden, hello."

"I'm looking for Dar. If you want to help, stay close and don't leave my side."

"Dar?" I called out to him, walking with Aden. I called out to Dar repeatedly and there was no response. I'm worried. He never went far from me or Aden. I crept through this long dark hallway. It seemed to never be used; there were spider webs all over the place. There was dust and old concrete floors, and rusted boards on the ground. I whispered Dar's name. There was no response. I opened the first door and the room was empty. I went to the second room on the left and it was an old bed that was made, and it seem like nothing had been touched for years.

"What are you doing in here?" I jumped and turned around.

"Aden. Geez, you scared me. I was looking for Dar. I just opened the door." I said while Aden walked ahead.

"He's in the front. I found him...this is my father's old room." He looked.

"I'm sorry, I didn't mean to..."

"It's okay." He said

"Let's go." He shut the door and we stood face to face. "

Is Dar okay?" My heart beats fast whenever he and I were so close.

"Do you always go in dark places looking for people, trying to help them?" he asked.

"That's how we met." I said sarcastically, but he wasn't amused.

"Let's get back to the other side." Aden said. There was a creaking sound. Aden's nose flared. He smelt something. "Something's here."

"Where?" I moved closer to him, as we both looked around. I was snatched from behind, "Aden." There was a high pitch screech, which you couldn't drown out by covering your ears. This creature held me close. His caved-in face was so horrible to look at, the eyes the size of a baseball, and teeth were like fangs. "Let go of me." I tried to push away. With one quick swoop as Aden chase the creature down, he kicked it and stabbed it with a green blade. It fell hard, and I landed on top of it. Its firm grip loosen. The blood from this creature was all over me. I pushed off of him. "Oh, grouse!"

"You okay?" Aden asked.

"Yeah!" I stood up.

"Let's get to the front with the others."

We walked all the way to the other side of the castle and Dar sat on the couch with a bandage on his arm and his leg. He was being interrogated by Kilen. He answered the same questions over and over again; it was like they didn't believe him. Dar needed to rest he was in no condition to be aggravated like he was.

"How many were there did you say?" Kilen asked.

"There are ten large She-ads in disguises." Dar said.

"How do you know the total?" Queen Patano asked.

"There are not just She-ads. There are Speed demons." Aden and I approached the others.

"What?" Queen Patano asked.

"It tried to take Gina." Aden said. "Dar, where were you when you were attacked?"

"I was standing outside of Gina's quarter. I never left her door my king." Dar held his cut shoulder.

"How many attacked you?" Kilen asked.

"Four She-ads. It seemed a distraction ritual was used against me." Dar added.

"No one but someone with phantom blood can do that." Queen Patano said.

"Did you recognize anyone?" Aden asked.

"What about a scent?" Kilen asked.

"Come on guys, give him a break." I said.

"We have to know this Gina." Aden said as he stared at me, noticing the burn across my side the fabric had melted badly... I said nothing. I knew he was trying to be sympathetic with me. "Does that hurt?"

"I'm fine." I lied. The burn stung like hell. In fact I didn't notice the pain until he pointed it out.

"Dar, what did they look like? If they are here, and we don't get a heads up on them, we are going into a war with trouble. Tell us. Try to remember." Ballajamen said.

"Oh for crying out loud, Could you remember if you've just gotten jumped by four huge creatures? Let him rest for a second and maybe you can get answers." I said.

"Gina is not safe in the open." Aden pointed at me without looking "Lilar, now" Aden said.

One minute they all were in front of me the next they weren't. I was in that concrete room again. This place was starting to be so chaotic, and I had been hating it. Thank God, Maggie and I were going home. I sat in this room for a while. Maybe hours. I stared at the wall. After a while Aden walked through it. I said nothing, I sat. He sat next to me. I stood up and walked away, and he followed.

"Is it time to go?" I asked.

"I'm going, but you're not." Aden said.

"You mean to tell me, you're going to leave me? Maggie only knows me. She will probably freak if she sees you again." I yelled.

"You have to stay in here, because we can't find these creatures, and this is the only place you're safe."

He said.

"Here in a room full of nothing. I will go crazy Aden…Don't do this. Please."

"I can't be on this mission and worrying about protecting you too."

"You don't have to protect me. Just let me get Maggie." I said.

"You need to be protected, you're too fragile. You can't go up against these things."

"Aden please. Wouldn't you worry about me being here? If someone has Phantoms blood, and used rituals or whatever wouldn't they be able to find me here?"

"You're right." Aden said, hating to agree.

"What about you? Wouldn't you worry? You won't be able to concentrate." I asked, he said nothing he walked out of the room. I yelled for Aden, and he appeared again from the wall, he called me to him with the wave of his hand. As soon as I took a breath, I stepped through the walls. Aden and I was either going to die on this rescue mission, or one of us wasn't going home. I wanted to touch him. I wanted to hold him and let him know how much I cared, but the proper thing to do was resist.

"When do you ever do what is proper?" Aden interrupted my thoughts as we walked.

"Wow, I'm sorry, you heard that."

"I know what you feel. Even if you don't speak it."

"How do I know what you feel, if you don't tell me?" I said.

"You don't. Let's keep it that way, okay?" He looked at me.

"Okay." We turned the hallway. I stopped, "What if I want to know?"

"I want you to know something. You can't always have what you want." Aden stood close.

"Just tell me, please. Before I leave here, Tell me how do you really feel about me?" Lady Nirew appeared right in front of us. Her face was puzzled and angry. She said nothing, but she snapped her fingers, and guards appeared and they transformed from regular servants to beasts and creatures, and She-ads. Aden had stood puzzled, but furious.

"Lady Nirew. What is this?" Aden asked looking at the creatures in a protective stance in front of me.

"Getting rid of our trouble. We would have been married and ruling this country together." Lady Nirew said.

"You betrayed me." Aden hands smoked. I looked at him and stepped back.

"I wouldn't have if you didn't bring her here. You both pushed me. I won't be anymore." Lady Nirew yelled. "And you, you leave me for eras to bring home a pet whose beauty is far worse than your own kind. I will kill her and her little friend, and we will marry. This country will be ours." She said

"Where's Maggie?" I asked.

"My father has her." Lady Nirew said.

"Ponchopalapare. You're his daughter?" Aden said through the clenching of his teeth.

"I knew you were one of them. Your arm at the festival, I couldn't quite figure it out." I said.

"Silence." Lady Nirew waved her arm and I flew back against the wall. I was pint, and She-ads gathered around Aden holding him down.

"Do you love her Aden?" She walked towards him. "I will make sure I will kill her personally."

"Don't touch her. I can't believe that I was going to marry a low living like you." Aden struggled with the She-ads. She clenched her fists causing Aden pain.

"And you, I bow to no one." Lady Nirew said in a mocking voice "You will kneel before me. She move her hands, whatever she did it made me fall to my knees, I struggled. I felt the pain, and I screamed it felt like my insides were being pulled out of me. "You are beneath me. Leash." A beast handed her a leash and she wrapped it around my neck.

"You will pay for this. I will make sure of it." I said on my knees.

"Quiet!" She said and kicked me and everything became dark.

****

After fighting with the She-ads I was finally out numbered. I was knocked unconscious and I came to. I was in this cave like atmosphere. I was tied to the walls. Gina was on the other side tied to another wall. She was still lifeless. I saw Maggie for the first time. She was in a glass case. She patted the glass trying to get Gina to wake up. When she seen me, she was cursing and screaming. I could barely hear her, but whatever she was saying, it wasn't pretty. I looked around no one was in sight. I notice I was able to break free. It seemed too easy, but I ran to Gina, trying to get her to wake up, and when she did, she was angry.

"Where is she?" Gina asked grabbing her head.

"I don't know. Maggie's there. You stay here, and I will get her out of there." I said.

"Okay." Gina waved at Maggie.

I walked quietly over to Maggie, and walked around the glass case, but I saw no way to get her out. The only way I could get her out was to shatter the glass. I told her to stand back. She was still cursing and screaming, but this time she pointing behind me. I turned around I was knocked away from the glass case. It was Lady Nirew. She had turned herself from what I always seen her as to a She-ad. I knew it was her from her scent of oils.

"Don't you dare?" Nirew said in a shaky voice.

"You lied from the beginning. You're the one with the phantoms blood." I stood ready for whatever she threw my way.

"My mother was a phantom…a pure breed. I will make you pay for what you've put me through. Starting with her life." She lifted her hand and a She-ad had Gina by the leash that was around her neck. She was being strangled.

"What do you want from me?" I asked her.

"I want you to marry me. I want us to be together like you promise me so many eras ago." Nirew said.

"We can't get married. Not after this." I said Gina struck the She-ad and she fell to the ground she ran over to me.

"You will marry me Aden. If it's the last thing you do." Lady Nirew yelled. The ground shook, and a howl came towards us. With every step the large creature took we felt.

"It's him." I said noticing that this creature killed my father. I must admit fear rose in me in the beginning but was quickly overcome with anger.

"Ponchopalapare." Gina said.

"Gina, get away from him." I heard Maggie scream.

"So we meet at last my young king." Ponchopalapare said.

"Better now, then never." My hands lit. The case Maggie was in filled with green liquid. The poison of a sapphire blade.

"Maggie." Gina ran towards her."

"Father I will deal with her. You make him regret the pain he has put me through." Lady Nirew said going after Gina.

"There's nothing left to say, what my daughter wants she gets." He said. "Your father ruined my life, but I will ruin his empire starting with you."

"It will never happen." I said. I ran to Ponchopalapare and we fought. This creature stood ten feet in the air. He had big hands and great stature. I swung and hit him, but he threw me down like a piece of paper. He would throw me, and I would get back up. This wasn't like training with Dar, and Kilen it's was much worse. It seemed that he memorized everything I did. My hands swelled with fire. I threw it at him, he would screech. I notice that I could affect him with fire, it was time for combat. I stood watching him; I was trying to discover all his weaknesses. Ponchopalapare was too tall to actually move at a speed like regular She-ads, but he was fast. I've never fought him, or ever encounter him before. I looked over at Gina, and she was trying to fight Nirew. Maggie was almost covered with the poison, I took a dagger I found on the floor, kicked it up with my feet and caught it and threw it at the glass case and it shattered. Maggie fell out of it coughing, and trying to get up, but you could tell she was still poisoned from the liquid.

"Gina, give her the medicine." I yelled.

"I will, just as soon as I get this thing off of me." Gina yelled back punching and struggling with Nirew, whom had turned to a She-ad permanently.

"Come here." Ponchopalapare grabbed me.

"Whoa!" I was lifted from the ground.

"You're no better than you father was."

"I'm just like my father." I said.

"Old and stupid?" he said; his arm was wrapped around my neck.

"No, fast and brilliant." I slipped out of his arms and attacked him, jumping off anything to get ahead of him in everything he did. He knew my moves because they were the same my father made. I had to re-strategize.

Chapter 16: The Battle

Nirew was huge and ugly. It was hard fighting her off. I had to get over to Maggie and give her the medicine. She had stopped moving. She lay sprawled on the floor. Nirew had me by the throat, her grip became tighter and tighter. I punched her, but it didn't faze her at all. I kneed her, and she went down. I ran to Maggie and stuck the syringe in her shoulder. Maggie coughed. Nirew dragged me away by my hair. I kicked and screamed, Maggie stood up weakly, and staggered towards me. She pushed Nirew and Nirew shoved her back. Maggie kicked her, and she flew back into a wall. Maggie was a trained black belt, and she had a few moves.

"I knew I should've taken those classes with you." I said.

"Oh no! Not Gina. You and I have a lot to discuss. How did you get me into this mess, and what are these things? And what's going on?" Maggie asked, coughing and trying to catch her breath.

"Long story." I half-smiled as Nirew ran towards us. Maggie screamed pulling me away from Nirew.

"We have to get out of here." Maggie was scared. She had no clue what was going on. She didn't even know that she wasn't on Earth anymore.

"Come here." Nirew grabbed me by the throat, lifting me from the ground. "You'll never have Aden."

"Gina." Maggie screamed. I don't know what happened, but suddenly she had courage she attacked Nirew.

"Let her go, you animal." She hit Nirew in the face and Nirew dropped me flying backwards.

"Thanks." I grabbed my neck.

"You take her high, I will get her low." Maggie said.

"Gotcha!" We ran towards Nirew. Maggie tackled her down, I fought like a girl, and Maggie was like a football player trained in the police academy. Nirew threw us off of her and changed from skin to She-ad. She was like a computer that had a glitch.

"I will get you out of this world if it's the last thing I do." Nirew stood over us and I heard Aden yelling. I looked towards him and he was hanging from the wall with a knife through him.

"Aden!" I screamed.

"He will die, and I will rule Sawdawa." Nirew laughed. An arrow flew threw her arm, and Queen Patano and Aden soldiers were there. Kilen and Ballajamen flew to help Aden. Dar attacked Nirew, but she flung him from her shoulders. Queen Patano recited words I couldn't understand she raised Nirew from the ground tossing her into the cave wall.

"Are you two okay?" Queen Patano asked.

"Yes." I said.

"What is going on Gina?" Maggie asked.

"Maggie this is Queen Patano and this is Maggie." I said.

"Hi." Maggie sound frighten looking at the Queen appearance.

"Finally we meet, I've heard a great deal about you." Queen Patano said. "Come, we must get you out of here and back to your world."

"What do you mean our world?" Maggie asked running behind Queen Patano.

"Long-story." I said "Wait Aden."

"You must go." Queen Patano said.

"I can't leave without saying goodbye." I saw Aden lying on the side with Soldiers standing around him, fighting off She-ads.

"You must, I will tell him, your farewells. I read your heart and mind from far away." Queen Patano said. Queen Patano held a blue stone in her hand. She held it tightly. The stone rose from her hand shining a bright light. The concrete from the wall chipped away falling casting a shape of a triangle. It swung open, making a sound of a bang. "Go now. Aden knows what you feel."

"No, I want to tell him one more time." I said.

"This portal will close. Gina, please you must leave." Queen Patano said.

"Gina let's go." Maggie said grabbing me as Queen Patano waved her hand motioning us to go through the portal. This oddly shape triangle looked like if you walked through, nothing would be on the other side. It looked like you would fall and nothing would be on the other side to catch you.

"Maggie, I can't leave him." I tried to pull away from her, but her grip was tight. Nirew had cut my arm with the arrow that went through her. I screamed. My arm bled. I turned towards her. Her hands filthy, she grabbed the cut and squeezed it. Queen Patano stepped in and fought her. I never knew that Queen Patano was a warrior and Queen. She fought hard, and she fought like it was the end for her. Dar helped fight Nirew, but she had hurt Dar. He was lying on the ground screaming at us to leave. He never yelled until now.

"Go through the portal." Queen Patano said.

"Gina let's go. Now" Maggie yelled. I walked to the portal, but I glanced at Aden. Kilen flew towards us and stood protecting us from flying objects.

"Go being. Go now." Kilen said.

"Please take me to Aden." I said, Kilen looked reluctant, but he glided me to him continue to block all objects.

Aden was injured. Blood ran down his mouth, I kneeled next to Aden, and he was holding his side. He said nothing. He laid there out of his mind. I wanted to rub his face, and he grabbed me, burning my arm. He thought I was going to attack him. I screamed when he opened his eyes, he let go, and he coughed up blood. Still he said nothing.

"Aden. Speak to me."

"Go home Gina." Aden said.

"I can't leave you like this."

"Go home. Please. I kept my promise to you. Go." He struggled to get his words out.

"I love you so much, please don't die. I will stay with you. I'll live here. I'll do whatever just, don't die." I cried. Aden stood and struggled to walk me towards the portal He fought off creatures attacking. It felt like the last time. I knew this was it.

"Go!" Aden said I was grabbed from behind and thrown across the room. "No." Aden yelled. I lay on the floor holding my head. Maggie stood me up and yelled. I couldn't understand what she was saying.

Queen Patano was fighting Nirew. It was a war, exactly what Aden had said it would be. I looked at Aden standing on his feet. He levitated himself in the air and spun around, he was like a live tornado and he slowly became fire. I was shocked.

"The portals open go Beings now, before it closes." Queen Patano lay on the ground with Nirew's dead body on top of hers.

Everyone would die, it was my entire fault. Aden fought hard against the lead She-ad, but it seems not to be enough. Everyone attacked Ponchopalapare, but he was too strong. The situation changed when Aden became angry. He burst into flames. He looked just like his father in his room. He flew straight through him with an Emerald dagger making him fall to his knees. Aden fell from the air. He stumbled next to me. Everyone was hurt barely holding themselves together. They were lying on the floor, dead, or pieces missing, but She-ads attacked.

"Gina. It's okay." Aden said.

"Thank you Aden." Maggie said "Gina let's go." The portal was almost closed we needed to leave now or never.

"This is the last time this portal can be opened for ten eras. Go now." Aden said, but then he stood in silence, as he looked down, the end of a blade was in his stomach. "Go, for it was not meant to be." He whispered from pain. He reached for my face and lightly touched it. I felt the heat, but I wanted it to burn just for the memory of how his skin felt against mine. "Gina, I love you." He pushed us through the portal.

"Aden." I yelled, but it was too late we were back at the hospital. The noise was deafening to come out of the portal.

"It's okay. Gina its okay." Maggie held me as I cried. Doctors ran into the room saying how they had been looking for us. They didn't know what happen to Maggie, and they had gathered around. There were more doctors and nurses around Maggie and me, looking at our bruises and cuts than you could count on one hand.

Chapter 17: Back to Earth

We had been back in our world for a year. At first all I thought about was Aden. Ponchopalapare had stabbed him right before he had pushed us through the portal. I had cried for weeks I had stop going to my classes, my life had really changed. Maggie and I had gotten our own apartment. I rarely came out of my room. She tried hard after I explained to comfort me, but she was angry with me. She continued school and worked. Then after a while, I went back to classes, worked. Occasionally I went out with Maggie. Nothing could change how I was feeling inside. I had killed the one guy I really loved. I think I see him every time I open my eyes. Everywhere I go I feel him watching me. I carry his cloak with me. I occasionally ride by the building I first met him. It's hard. Maggie tries not to talk about him, and she gives me my space.

"Gina, are you hungry?" Maggie asked.

"No, not really." I said.

"Eat something." She said.

"I'm not hungry." I said.

"How long are you going to do this?" Maggie asked.

"Do what?" I ignored her concerns.

"Why don't you hang out with your new friend? Andrew really likes you. Call him." Maggie smiled.

"I have already talked to him. It's kind of hard for me." I said.

"Why? What's wrong with him?" Maggie asked.

"It's hard for me not to think of Aden. I can't stop thinking I'm doing something wrong." I looked out of the window.

"You said that you think he's dead, but I don't think so."

"Okay, that makes me feel even worse."

"Why Gina? He can't come here for years." Maggie said.

"I know, but it's just I miss him." I said.

"Just give Andrew a chance." Maggie said touching my hand so I could turn her way.

"Okay, well I have a little confession to make."

"Okay." Maggie said.

"I'm going out with him, and we have been dating for months," I smiled.

"How could you not tell me?"

"Because you get excited over dates. I wanted to do this for me. Slowly." Maggie pulled me to my room.

"Hey, I don't act crazy like that." We laughed. "How could you keep that big of a secret from me?"

"Uh, you do. And it was something I didn't want to get pushed into until I was ready to go out." I laughed. "I'm actually going to meet him now, so I have to go."

"So much for company tonight." Maggie laughed. "Go have fun, and I will see you later."

"I will make it up to you." I said walking out of the house.

I got into my car to meet with Andrew for dinner. I met him in very beautiful restaurant. I walked over to the table and Andrew stood six feet tall, slender and built. His hair was cut short and black. His skin was pale, and he had beautiful green eyes. He pulled out the chair for me, and kissed me before I sat down. I must admit, It gave me chills every time, and it wasn't a good thing.

"You look….incredible!" Andrew starred at me.

"Thank you, you look good yourself." I smiled at him.

"How did you get away from your friend tonight?" He laughed.

"I told her about us. So she's cool. She respects my boundaries."

"See, there was nothing to worry about. You should have told her earlier." Andrew said.

"Andrew, she knows now. I know you wanted me to tell her sooner, but now you can come meet her. And stay at my place when you want." I said touching his hand.

"I like that idea. I will take you up on that tonight." He smiled.

"Good." I said holding my head.

"What's wrong honey?" Andrew asked.

"I have a slight headache, but I'm okay." I smiled.

"Well, my job will cause me to be out of town for a while."

"Where are you going?" I asked curiously.

"Um, Switzerland!" Andrew said, and something about his posture was off.

"Wow, really. What's there?" I asked.

"It's government business baby. I can't really discuss it with you." He weaseled his way out of it, looking at his menu.

"I understand." Looking at the menu.

"Are you ready to order?" The waiter sound so familiar. I glanced up. My vision went blurry. It was like I was seeing through his soul. It freaked me out, and I jerked.

"Are you okay?" Andrew asked.

"Yes." I tried to focus on the menu.

"Can you give us a minute?" Andrew asked the waiter.

"Yes, sir." The waiter walked away.

"Steak and potatoes sound good." Andrew said.

"Yes they do." I said seconds later I couldn't see anything but a white light. I saw this woman with a white cloak. She whispered my name. I jumped.

"What's wrong? You ok? Andrew asked and my vision focused on him.

"Yes, I need to eat something that's all. I have a headache and it is getting bad. I'm sorry." I drank a glass of water. I heard my name whispered. I looked around, but I saw no one.

"Maybe we should go." Andrew said.

"Is that ok?" I asked. "I'm sorry."

"No it's fine." We walked out of the restaurant and I heard my name again. The call became very aggressive. I turned, bumping into a car. Then light sight through my eyes, and I saw a woman reaching for me. I screamed, falling to the ground.

"Ah, what's wrong? Baby. What's going on?" Andrew lifted me up as I looked around breathing fast.

"I need to get home." I said.

"Let me drive, you may have an accident driving like this." Andrew sat me in the passenger seat of my car.

As we drove I kept my eyes opened, afraid of what I might see if I close them again. Andrew got me through the door, and to my room. He whispered with Maggie in the hallway. It wasn't much of a whisper. He was frank and said "She had a headache and freaked." They stood watching me, I could feel it. Maggie tapped me.

"Here let me help you change, so you can relax." Maggie said.

"I'm fine. I don't want to move." I said.

"Honey let her help you. I will wait out here." Andrew said.

"Ok." I muttered.

I changed, and laid in the bed and Andrew came in afterward and lay next to me. He said nothing, he just rubbed my arms. He lay quietly until I slept. I awakened in the morning and Andrew was asleep with his arm wrapped around me. I turned to him, waking him.

"Hey." Andrew said.

"Hi, did you stay here all night for me?" I smiled.

"For you, no I stayed for me." He laughed giving me a small kiss. "I'm going to talk to Maggie ok."

"Go ahead; I have to make a few calls."

"Ok." I said walking to the kitchen where I smelled freshly brewed coffee.

"Hey you!" Maggie said.

"Hi. Coffee smells good."

"Gina what happened last night?" Maggie whispered. We were trying to be discrete with our conversation.

"I don't know. Do you think Aden is trying to…?" I whispered.

"No. Don't start this. Aden may not be dead. But he is not trying to appear again. And if he is too bad, move on. You can't keep hurting yourself like this." Maggie whispered aggressively.

"I saw something. I can't explain." I said looking around making sure our surroundings were clear.

"What if he's not dead? Are you going to leave Andrew? He seems like a great guy." Maggie said.

"He is. No, I will not leave him. It's been a year." I said.

"Well, try to focus. Don't let whatever that is freaking you out ruin this." Maggie said. "If Aden's anything like you described, he will be fine."

Maggie for more than once in our life was right. Aden should be king, and I should live my life on earth. I don't think he would freak me out if he was trying to contact me. I pray I was just tired. My life was very different after a year. I missed Aden, and I loved him very much. But what was I supposed to do now? I had Andrew. I didn't want to lose him at all. I wanted to leave Nexima behind me.

Aden

Heir to the Throne

Epilogue

A New Beginning

"So, where were you?" Maggie asked.

"What's on the agenda today?" I ignored her question.

"The top priority on the agenda is to know where you have been three mornings in a row."

"Maggie!" I sighed.

"You are doing the walk of shame. Same clothes from last night." Maggie said pointing to my clothing.

"Ah! So, we are looking for me an apartment right?"

"Gina!" Maggie sighed.

"No details. No questions. We will talk about this another time. Let's have me and you time." I said

"You are not right, at all."

"I love you, but can we please not do this."

"Spill!"

"No."

"Fine."

"Thank you."

"At least say you had a good time." She gave a devilish smile

"Maggie."

"Okay, okay." Maggie said. "Are you going to live in the same area or are we looking somewhere else.

I heard nothing she said, my mind was on so many different things. Especially things Maggie wanted nothing to do with.

"What's wrong Gina?" Maggie asked.

"I'm still having those dreams." I said.

"Are you? Maybe it's because you think of that place all the time. You have got to let it go." Maggie whispered.

"I'm trying to. It's like it's a message trying to come to me or something."

"That's it. Let's go." Maggie said.

"What are you doing?" I asked as Maggie pulled me.

"Keep the change." Maggie gave the waiter the money and dragged me out of the bakery. "Look there."

"Where?" I looked.

"Across the street." We stood on the sidewalk looking. "That's the building. It's been turned into the arts center for the school, and it's opened all day and night. He's not coming back."

It just hit then with all the memories of last year.

"Let it go. I'm tired of it." Maggie stormed away.

"Maggie. Why are you so frustrated?"

"I'm trying to moved pass it, but you are getting bombarded with all this stuff. It's driving me crazy. He's gone Gina. He's gone. He's not coming back."

"Maggie. I'm not trying to bring him back. I'm just telling my best friend what's going on with me."

"As your best friend, I'm telling you to ignore it and keep it pushing forward. I'll see you at home." Maggie walked away.

"Nice breakfast."

"It should have been." Maggie got in her car and drove away. I went home and waited for Maggie, but she called and said she was at work and would be late. I knew that it was something going on I just didn't want to tell her anything else. It was something weird. I couldn't explain. I didn't know what to think. Maggie had enough of my problems for the last year. I laid down for a second it seemed. I was seeing things. I opened my eyes and I was standing on the edge of the balcony. I had cuts and bruises on my arms. I turned around and I saw white cloaks go by. I walked slowly in the house and whatever it was stood covered from head to feet. It looked up at me and it had red eyes.

"Aden." I whispered.

"I am far from Aden." It said and disappeared. I shook my head clear when I heard Maggie open her room door.

"Are you okay?" Maggie asked walking into the hallway.

"I'm seeing things." I said.

"Gina. You're cut what happened?"

"I don't know Mag." I looked at my arms.

"Geez Gina! I think you are going to need to seek therapy." She said nursing my wounds.

"I'm not crazy. I woke up like this." I snapped.

"You need to go back to bed and get some sleep and be careful."

"Yea. I will." I said grabbing my bandaged arms. I walked to my room, and the pain from the cuts kicked in. I was wondering, where they came from. Someone was here, and whoever it was gave me the scars to prove it.

I awaken with a headache the next morning and I searched through the hall way closet for aspirin and then it hit me. *Gina! Gina! Gina!* I heard my name. I looked around and seen nothing, but my name kept being whispered.

"How did you sleep G.?" Maggie asked.

"Good." I said as my name was called repeatedly. My vision became cloudy and then it cleared. I saw a bright white light. I couldn't focus. The pain shot through my head. I heard a huge thud; my hands quickly reached my head. The vision became a little clear. It was a white cloak again, this time running away. I screamed and fell to the floor. The pain was intense. There was burning, I felt myself shaking.

"Gina. Sweetie." Maggie screamed.

"Stop it, stop it, stop it." I yelled. I saw many trees, and I heard a woman scream.

"What's wrong? Gina, what's wrong?" Maggie shook me clear out of the dream like vision I was having.

"I don't know." I was breathing hard, my eyes were closed tightly. I wouldn't open my eyes in fear of what I might see. "Someone's here."

"Open your eyes; no one is here, but you and I. Calm down. You're shaking. Open your eyes." I opened my eyes slowly. "Gina."

"What?" I said looking around checking my surroundings and then looking at Maggie.

"Your eyes!" Maggie said covering her mouth.

"What's wrong with them?" I stood and looked into the hallway mirror.

"They're yellow." Maggie responded

We both stood very silently. I looked in the mirror mesmerized as Maggie looked back and forth at me and in the mirror.

Something was wrong and something weird was definitely happening. I had a very bad feeling in the pit of my stomach. I thought all the odd things in my life were really over, but now it seems they were beginning again.

Author's Notes

Born a Detroit, Michigan native it was hard growing up, but my parents instilled in me the most important things in life; God, Family and Education. I always pushed to be the best I could be even if I fell most of the time. With five other siblings in the household it was a challenge. I lost a brother at a young age of twelve, moved to Vegas with my parents and younger brother and continued life there, learning for the first time many cultures and variations of life. I always loved reading and writing, that's all I did. I had tons of journals. I also won creative writing awards. At the age of sixteen I moved back to Michigan and at the age of seventeen years old I became ill with viral meningitis. A illness the hospital said that Tylenol would help and would be gone in a week, but sadly it didn't. The illness progressed and turned into Encephalitis causing swelling on my brain making me not remember things, barely walking and talking. With the swelling, it later left a scar on my brain causing me to become epileptic and having a mood disorder, short-term memory loss and slurred speech. Doctor's said I would never be the same, and that I would never read a book or be normal again. But, I beat the odds with God's and my family help. I graduated from high school and college with an Associate of Arts degree. I have shelves full of books that I have read and completed but best of all I wrote a book. Through all of my trials I climbed those mountains and jumped those hurtles, and you can too. –Tiffany Y.